Tattooed Angel

Tattooed Angel

C. J. Abbot

Midnight Whistler Publishers – since 1979

First Edition

ISBN-13:
978-0615446967
(Midnight Whistler Publishers)

ISBN-10:
0615446965

Midnight Whistler
http://www.midnightwhistler.com
info@midnightwhistler.com

To Greg Heet, whose warehouse on Ducommon Street in Los Angeles inspired the setting for this book.

Rain

The rain beat down on Los Angeles as if it meant to pound the city flat. It was surreal, a work of art with ugliness replacing beauty, discordance replacing harmony. Shawn Cauver drove through the deserted warehouse district as if for the first time, though he had done this drive every day for months. Yet here he was, threading his way between the drab, gray structures.

"Getting a place down here seemed like a good idea once, but today, not so much," thought Shawn, shaking his head, wishing he was home already with a warm soup in his hands.

It was his uncle's idea. "You work downtown, you might as well live downtown," he said. "That way, you don't have the traffic to contend with."

"Still, on a Friday in a cloud burst," thought Shawn, "he's got a point. I could be stuck on the freeway, I suppose."

Now here he was on the empty streets in a forgotten part of L.A. in one of the worst rains of the season, visibility zero. The rain fell so hard the wipers, showing too much neglect, couldn't handle it. Shawn couldn't see enough through the windshield to know where he was.

"Great!" Shawn said aloud. "I might be right outside my place and not know it."

The larger building on the right seemed familiar, but all else was uniform gray in the darkness of a stormy afternoon. He slowed to see if he could read an address, or even find an address to read in this neglected section of town. The workers who came in crammed in cars or walking from the bus stop didn't care about the streets or buildings; it was someone else's to worry about. The managers who came to manage the workers didn't care, that was for the owners; they got all the money anyway. The owners never came here; it was depressing. They didn't earn enough from their businesses to make them come down to a depressing place.

So, the walls didn't get repainted, the sidewalks didn't get swept and broken windows got boarded over but never fixed. The result was a solid wall of gray from the street to the buildings and today, all the way to the sky. Lost amid the gray, Shawn could distinguish nothing. He urged the aging Toyota through the potholes and dips, pausing at the stop sign only because he wasn't sure what street he was on.

A crash on his hood made him jump. Had he hit someone? No, someone had hit him. There was someone out there who had just run into his car from the side, someone small. Was it a child?

Shawn squinted, hoping it would help bring the offending person into focus. To his surprise, it was a girl, a soaking wet girl. She lurched to the passenger side door of his car and pulled on the handle. The door was locked, so she banged on the window with a fist, her face contorted. Shawn hit the door-unlock without thinking and the girl pulled the handle, jumped in the front seat and slid down to the floor. There she lay, wet and shivering.

Many things registered with Shawn. One: the girl was afraid, quivering with fear as well as cold. Another was she must have been running, as she was out of breath. The third and perhaps most notable thing: she was stark naked.

Another body appeared through the rain, this one a man, large and hooded. Over his left arm was a yellow robe, fluttering in the stiff wind like a colored flag. In his right hand was a pistol and he pointed it through the windshield. He moved to the passenger door of Shawn's car and reached for the handle.

From a distance behind came a series of sharp sounds: pistol-cracks. Gunshots were common enough in this neighborhood. The man was immediately distracted and ran in the direction of the shots. Shawn stepped on the gas and went around the next corner, scanning for a landmark, something to guide him home.

The girl was small and folded up on the floor of the front seat, clutching her shoulders with the cold. Her hair was black, tangled and dripping wet. She looked up at him, her eyes pleading for mercy and kindness.

She was Asian, with a tiny, Japanese face like on a cola ad, only with blue lips. She was cold. On her back was an outline of a tree with flowers, some of which looked recently inked.

Lights appeared in the rear-view mirror. Shawn glanced at the girl; the large eyes went wider still as she felt the presence of another car. The lights swung around in a wide u-turn, heading back toward the gunfire.

Shawn reached into the back seat, grabbed his jacket and threw it over the girl cowering next to him. He pushed the heat up to full and directed the brunt of it to the floor. A slender hand found the edge of the coat and pulled it closer.

The building on the corner with the blue, faded awning was familiar, so he turned the corner and sped down two blocks to the warehouse he called home, at least for the last three months. In the road ahead, headlights appeared, coming fast. Shawn maintained speed, trying to look casual.

"No one is ever here at this hour," thought Shawn, "especially on a Friday, getaway-day." The car sped passed him; heads turned to regard him behind dark, tinted glass.

"A black car with darkened windows—how L.A. can you get?" he thought.

3

In the rear-view mirror, he saw the car go through the intersection and around the corner, too fast and too wide. At least they weren't stopping him to do a search.

At the garage door, he pulled up close, regretting not getting an automatic opener when he had the chance, but this was not a time for recriminations. He sprinted from the car to the door, key in hand, trying to work the lock, his hands shaking; the rain pelting him. When he got the lock open, he pulled upwards on the handle, rolling the great door back, then jumped into the car and pulled it into the warehouse. Once inside, he returned to the roll-up door and jumped for the handle, using his whole weight to pull it down. On the ground Shawn huddled, shaking, still holding the door handle. His heart beat out a samba in his chest and his breath was fast and shallow.

At the sides of the door were interior locks, two pegs to shove in through the side of the door and into the wall. Shawn looked up, as if to make sure they were still there, then leaped up. He shoved the right peg in place, then the left. He stood back to see his handiwork.

"That should hold them!" he thought. No one could open the door from the outside with the pegs in. Of course, he hoped no one would try. With any luck they were all chasing the sound of gunfire.

Shawn became aware of the engine still running behind him, and the wet, naked girl huddled in his front seat.

The Girl

In the car, a frightened face peeked from beneath the jacket like a kitten saved from drowning. Shawn turned off the engine and closed the driver side door. At the passenger side, he opened the door and extended a hand.

"Come on, let's get you warmed up," he said.

The girl rolled onto the seat and pulled the fabric of the jacket around her, upside down and not quite working right, but better than nothing. She unfolded herself from the seat and stepped out onto the cold, concrete floor of the warehouse with a foot still sore from running down the roughest streets in L.A. The second foot followed. She winced as she tried to stand.

"Here, let's try this," said Shawn, reaching one arm under her legs and the other around her back. She lifted her arm around his shoulders and let him take her, leaning into him as if she had been praying for someone to carry her away.

Shawn had no difficulty cradling the small girl in his arms as if she were a child. She was not a child. The jacket couldn't hide it.

Up the wide, wooden stairs to the second floor, Shawn assessed the situation out loud, speaking to the girl.

"OK, I don't think anyone saw us come in here. I passed a couple of cars and some people on foot, but none of them were around when we pulled in. They could guess a car disappeared somewhere in these streets, but there are hundreds of warehouses in this part of town, so it could have been any one of them."

The girl didn't respond; her eyes were closed and he wondered if she had gone unconscious.

On the second floor, he went to the bathroom in the corner. The bath tub was an afterthought to the décor, so it was not so much in the bath room as out in the open—a moot point since he lived alone—until now. He set the naked girl on the chair and started the water running. His robe hung by the tub on a shiny new hook screwed into an ancient wood support, picturesque and full of character. He threw the robe around her, pulling the soft terrycloth over her legs, hiding her small breasts and slim frame from view. He sighed to do so, but she was cold; his assessment of her beauty would have to wait. She opened her eyes and gratitude poured out of them.

"Aha! Awake, eh?" He tried to sound casual, as if this happened all the time. It didn't. The girl smiled, so he continued: "My name is Shawn. Pleased to meet you. This was my uncle's place. He let me have it when I got a job downtown. He said, 'You work downtown, may as well live downtown.' It's a caretaker arrangement. He likes having me here to take care of things until he can sell it and make a profit. The way the economy's going, it could be a while, so I have a place until then. That's good, because besides a place to live I have my own private workshop for a couple of projects I'm working on. But that's for another time. Right now, I'm running you a bath, it'll warm you up."

Shawn chattered without a plan or direction, but so what? It was a desperate time calling for desperate measures. Clearly the usual rules didn't apply.

"Once you're warmed up, I'll find some socks and a tee shirt, you can climb into bed and I'll make soup. Do you like soup? I have lots of soup. It's easy to make and ... and I'm talking too much. Let me get some light on the subject."

He reached for the light, then stopped, looking to the windows.

"No, if they see a glow, they'll know someone's here."

The electrical system had been shot when he moved in, so he put it on a power-saver system. Each segment of the loft was on a separate master switch. To turn on power to the TV or radio, there was a switch. To turn on the lights, there was a master switch. The switch in the kitchen ran power to all the counter appliances. Without the master switches on, the place was dark and the meter in the back, set outside for easy reading, was still.

A look to the tub showed it was filling, with steam rising from the water.

"OK, let's get you in here and warmed up, what's say?"

The girl raised her arm and bent her knees welcoming him to lift her again. He left the robe behind, letting it drop to the floor, and carried her to the tub.

The tub was small so he could never get his knees and shoulders wet at the same time, but the girl seemed lost in it. The water completely covered her. Shawn stood there a moment, admiring her nakedness under the guise of making sure the level of the water was perfect.

She huddled forward, dipping her small breasts into the water. He could see the half-drawn tree across her back and a pang of guilt shot through him. She was in pain and all he could do was to leer at her. He took a wash cloth and dipped it into the water, running it over her back. She winced but endured it. When he finished she sat back and closed her eyes.

"Is the temperature all right? Not too hot?"

The eyes opened, black, large and lovely. She sighed. Shawn took it as a yes and turned the water off. Less pleasing tasks demanded his attention.

"I won't be far, just fixing a few things." Shawn tore himself away from his naked guest rather than sit and stare at her. He bit his lip and shook all over, taking a deep breath for the next thing, whatever the next thing was.

"Oh, yeah! Soup," he said, turning toward the kitchen.

The warehouse was large and empty, wooden and old, with dust everywhere. To get it ready to move in, there had been two days of sandblasting and three days of cleanup to get the dust and dirt out. The effect on the wooden beams was like driftwood, artistic and grainy.

The skylight in the center of the loft space allowed for moonlight to be filtered in. A few strategically placed lamps and some track lighting would surely set a mood transforming the drab warehouse into a picturesque artist's loft. But to date, the only available light was from the large, industrial-strength fixtures on the ceiling. He created the effect he wanted with designer candles from the boutique near work; expensive, but cozy. With a CD playing and dinner in progress, the atmosphere was downright romantic. Now, of course, it was dark and cold, but light in the windows would give them away.

A glance to the street showed the rain was still strong, but the roads were empty. Large curtains had been hung to protect the windows from the sand blasting a few weeks earlier. He was glad he waited before taking them down. He pulled them closed, shutting the night out.

Down in the street, a car drove by, the lights on and the windows darkened. Someone searched for this girl; this naked, half-tattooed girl. Deep inside, Shawn knew he would never let them get their hands on her again.

The loft's rear windows looked over the roof covering the back half of the first floor, but they were still visible from the alley. He looked once at the empty alley and closed the curtains again.

Outside, the storm raged, the rain beating a steady tempo on the roof. The wind drove the rain into the windows, but the windows showed only blackness and gave no hint of life inside; just another dark and empty warehouse among dozens of dark and empty warehouses.

The door to the downstairs had never been closed, but he closed it now. Better than to cover the downstairs windows; which might be a tip-off to those doing the searching. It was better to look empty and abandoned.

The door creaked and offered some resistance, but it gave in and finally shut tight. The glass on the door had been painted over. It was on his list to scrape the paint off, but now he was glad he had neglected the list.

No sound came from the tub and fear instantly rose up inside him. He picked up the candle by the couch, struck a match and touched it to the wick. In the tub, a small head covered in wet, black hair was turned toward him, watching his progress. Shawn breathed a sigh, not sure what he had thought, maybe she had slipped unconscious under the water. He was glad she had not.

The small stool from the kitchen made a good table for the candle by the tub and he brought out several other similar candles, scented and colored—ornamentation for his colorful lifestyle. He put the candles onto glass dishes, all from Pottery Barn, and lit them, filling the warehouse loft with strange shadows.

"How about tomato soup?" Shawn looked around to the tub, hoping there might be a slight smile on her cherubic face. The look was expectant, or perhaps disbelieving. "Or chicken, chicken soup might be better. Yes, chicken soup—better."

He took down a can of hearty chicken soup and turned toward the electric can opener, stopping long enough to realize he only had candlelight. A manual can opener was in the drawer and it occurred to him he had never used it since he moved in—it was a relic from the old college days. He produced a saucepan and before long the smell of chicken-noodle was in the air.

"Better?" Shawn asked the pixie in his bath tub.

She nodded.

"OK! Let's get you out and dried off, then settled in with a hot bowl of soup."

He pulled the plug and held up a bath sheet, trying not to stare. She stood and let him pat the water from her body, then wrap her in the robe and lift her out of the tub.

Once in the bed, he wrapped her hair in a towel and propped her up using every pillow he had.

Shawn inspected her feet, which were, in fact, badly cut and bruised. There were also cuts and bruises on her hands and knees. She had clearly fallen several times while running. Bruises began to show on her face and shoulders, indicating she had been beaten as well.

"Someone has treated you badly. I would never."

The large eyes looked up like a frightened puppy as she pulled the covers up to her chin. Shawn got a bowl of soup and sat by her on the bed, lifting the spoon to her mouth. As she ate, he chattered on in a one-sided conversation.

"There's no one around on the weekends, which is good and bad. On one hand, it's quiet and no one bothers me. On the other hand, the pizza guy doesn't want to come here, so no sense ordering delivery. There's enough to keep me busy and it's good to be doing physical projects. I mean, I sit and stare at a screen all week at work, so getting my hands dirty with real life is a welcome break. I work for Tickleme.com, a search engine with an auction site and swap program. It's interesting and could lead to something. The pay is okay and they'll give me an interest in the company once we get off the ground."

The girl's eyes looked up; the frightened, trusting, puppy-look winning him over completely, making him forget she was in his bed and, other than a thin terrycloth robe, completely nude.

"Um! Let's see. I'm single, a college graduate and play guitar, not well, but enough. I'm working on a new thing for the guitar, but it's just a prototype at this point. Um, I drive a Toyota and work at a dot-com. Somehow, I thought there would be more to me, but apparently there isn't."

The angel in his bed looked at him, her little eyebrows knitting together. Whether it was something he said or the soup no longer flowing, he didn't know. Covering his bases, he continued spooning soup.

"But enough about me. I'm boring and dull. You, on the other hand, must be an interesting person. I mean, you have a tree tattooed to your ..."

A frown crossed her face and her eyes dipped.

"It's a beautiful back and it's a good tree, though that must have hurt."

The girl nodded. Yes, it had hurt. And he got the distinct impression she didn't choose to get the tattooShe didn't walk in with some girlfriends, tipsy, and say, "I think I'll get a tree, one that covers my whole back." No, this was someone's idea, but not hers.

"Look, I'm sorry. But you're here now. I won't let them hurt you."

Her tiny mouth spread into a small smile, then opened to receive a spoonful of soup.

"So, you speak English?"

She smirked, gave a tiny, childish laugh and nodded.

"Well, you haven't really said anything yet, so I only assumed."

She swallowed, looked at him and whispered, "Yes, I speak English. Thank you for the soup." Her voice was strained. The events of the evening had exhausted her. Shawn was just glad the man with the pistol hadn't found her first.

"You're welcome," was all he said, though he wanted to scoop her up and hold her, to protect her from all the badness in the world.

For a while, they sat in silence: Shawn spooning soup into the girl who ran naked into his car, her looking up at him like he was her savior and could do no wrong. Where had she come from? There were Japanese companies downtown, she could have come from any of them. She could have come from one of the many empty warehouses. Out of one, into another—frying pan into the fire. Except he wasn't going to force her to get tattooed or beat her black and blue.

The eyes lost focus and closed as the last spoonful of soup disappeared into her lips, now pink and full.

"You're tired. I understand. You rest. I'm going to see to your feet." Shawn leaned over and kissed her on the forehead, lingering with his lips on her brow. In that moment, he wanted even more to hold her, not as a lustful lover, but as a protector.

Remembering the task at hand, he brought out gauze and ointment and sat at the end of the bed, soothing and wrapping her feet. As he did, she drifted off and in no time, she relaxed and breathed the regular, shallow tempo of a sleeping baby.

As she slept, he slipped a pair of socks over her gauze wrapped feet and tucked them under the covers. The girl let out a sigh. Shawn sat there beside the bed and watched her sleep.

Horishi

Earlier the same day, the horishi arrived at his assignment. The back room of the night club was drab and dark. Turning on the light didn't make the place look any better. It was private, which was was the main concern. Still, the horishi was hesitant to put his bag down, he didn't know what might be on the floor. Cleanliness was a concern, at least to him; he was a professional, after all.

"This is where you'll work," the big man said.

Carlo Rossini wore a black overcoat, protection from the rain outside. Beneath it was a three-piece black suit and beneath, the horishi knew, was a Glock nine-millimeter.

"It's not clean," the horishi said. The man was immaculate, his shirt was laundered and pressed, with pants holding a crease in the rain and polished shoes. He was also rail-thin and clearly Japanese. Rossini could not pronounce the horishi's name. He covered by not addressing him directly. He spoke to a man standing at the door.

"Clean it up. Get some guys in. Clean off the table and make sure the light works."

"Tebori means to tattoo by hand. It is an ancient art. I'm not putting a heart on a sailor's arm, I'm going to make a work of art to fascinate everyone who has the honor to gaze upon it. Sujibori alone, the outline of the piece, will take weeks."

Rossini broke his own rule and addressed the man directly.

"You have two days. Outline as you go. If I don't see the start of a memorable work of art by the end of the day, I'll get a new artist."

13

The tattoo artist sighed.

"Vine of Knowledge and Honor will be easiest, not much color or detail. I'll have it for you. But I'll need a larger light." He knew the act of getting a new artist included getting rid of the old one. He would sacrifice art for life, his ancestors would understand.

"You'll have it." The big man walked out, leaving the horishi alone in the room. The horishi bit his lip and let his shoulders slump, then straightened up and took stock of his surroundings. At least the big man was gone.

Rossini walked into the empty night club and up to the two men sitting on stools at the bar, wishing there were beers in front of them.

"Where is this girl? Do we have her yet?"

"The boyfriend's bringing her in," said one of the men. He was thin, with a receding hairline and a goatee. He looked lost in the shirt, which was too big for his neck. He was an idiot, Rossini knew, but he was also a cousin. Business and family went together in his world.

"When?" asked Rossini, clearly unhappy with the explanation so far.

"Any time now. She'll be here," said the cousin. The other one sat slouched, watching the exchange, wondering in what way it would work against him.

"I don't like it from the beginning. The man's rich, his parents are flush. Why are we doing this?"

The big man searched the floor at his feet for an answer. There was none there. The cousin didn't have an answer either. He shrugged and turned back to the bar, still devoid of beer.

At the front door a young man appeared. He was dressed in a dark tee shirt, a tan sport coat and blue jeans. With him was a young Japanese girl in a stylish pants-suit and pony-tail. The big man looked up.

"What's this? Are they closed?" asked the girl.

"I just have to talk to this guy," said the man.

He brought the girl to Rossini, putting a hand in the small of her back as he did. He shoved the girl at the big man, who raised a hand to the two men at the bar. They stood and walked over to the girl, taking her by the arms, one man to each arm.

"There!" said the young man. "Now we're square?"

"That was the arrangement," said the big man.

"Kevin? What's going on?" the young girl cried out, as the two men took hold of her.

Kevin turned around and retraced his steps to the door, trying not to look eager to leave. But he was eager to leave, to put the whole thing behind him, to just forget it and start again.

He would have to say he had a fight with his girlfriend and she left after harsh words. He would box up her things and say she took them with her. He would put them into his storage locker, then his car trunk, then a dumpster downtown. He had it all planned out.

He only had a day to put his plan together, but he was sure he was in the clear. This would take care of his debt and he would be free of it. There was no other way. If he had not turned her over to the big man, they would have contacted his family and he would have been ruined. They had proof of his drug abuse and his gambling problem. Now he would have to be squeaky-clean, but at least he would be free of the debt. Four hundred-thousand dollars is a lot of bad luck to cover. In Southern California, girlfriends come and go.

"Kevin?" the girl screamed. "Kevin, come back! What's happening? Who are these people? What have you done?"

Her voice stilled as a needle went into her arm. She collapsed into the arms of the other man.

"Take her in back, there's a table there. Strip her and lay her down on it. The tattoo guy is back there. Cochran wants her marked."

The big man watched as the two other men carried the drugged girl into the back room. He twisted his mouth and walked to the bar. Taking a large bottle from below the bar, he poured two fingers into a heavy-bottomed glass. He downed the drink in one gulp and slammed the glass on the bar with a loud bang.

"I hate this whole deal," he said, not too loud.

At the end of the day, Rossini walked back into the back room to find a whimpering girl strapped, face down, to the high work table. The horishi, the tattoo artist, worked white into the pedals between the shoulder blades. The lower part of the tree was sketched in, the lowest part done in sketching pen, the outline, the Sujibori.

The art of Tebori, tattooing by hand instead of electric needle, can be a time-consuming process but the horishi worked well with the simple design. The girl was not so drugged as before, she showed signs of life, waking up to the worst of situations: she was naked, strapped face-down to a table and a needle being inserted into her skin, leaving there for all time a picture she knew nothing about. The Vine of Knowledge and Honor looked more like a thin dogwood tree, but the horishi worked quickly; it was not likely anyone knowledgeable would see it and call him on the rendition.

Outside, the rain came down; the day grew dark. The storm grew worse as night fell. The horishi was tired

"We should take a break, we have been going all day," said the horishi, putting down his pen. He stretched, causing his back to pop several times. The girl whimpered something unintelligible.

"What's that, little lady?" asked the big man, leaning over close.

"Bathroom, please." The voice was weak, barely a whisper.

"Sure, why not. You've been getting the needle all day, you're due."

He reached for a robe laying over the chair at the end of the table, bright yellow with a Bonsai tree embroidered on the back. He laid a white, gauze cloth over the back of the girl and then put the robe over her. He removed the straps from her wrists and ankles.

The girl struggled to her feet, faltered once and fell into the horishi. He steadied the girl and aimed her toward the bathroom toward the back of the room.

The girl stood before the dirty mirror looking at her face, tangled hair, and bare shoulders. She turned, looking at the gauze across her back wondering what it was hiding. She pulled the robe up and tied it around her. Her eyes hardened in the mirror and she looked to the window. It was closed, but not locked. The bars on the window outside were held by screws but the wood was old and rotted.

She placed the hook on the door into the eye, opened the window and pushed hard on the bars. They gave way, falling into the street on the other side. She stepped up on the toilet, then the sill, and out onto the concrete. She began running, away from the club, not sure where she would go.

The noise brought the big man to the door. He tried the door and found it latched. He put his shoulder to it and it sprang open without a fight, sending the latch flying across the tiny toilet room and ricocheting around the walls. He stepped to the window and plunged his head out, looking to the left and to the right. Rain pelted his head as he saw the bright yellow robe fluttering around the corner.

17

"Damn!" he shouted, pulling back from the window and pushing the horishi out of his way as he ran out of the back room and through the empty night club, followed by his two henchmen.

"Get the car, cut her off! Call the other guys, get them all out! I want that girl!"

The big man wasn't slow as you might think, he covered the ground quickly, his Glock appearing in his right hand. He ran the small, barefoot girl down in the course of two blocks. He reached out a hand and grabbed the collar of the yellow robe, pulling it to him, expecting to have her. The robe fell free, hanging loose in his hand. He stepped on the sash and tripped, falling face first into the street and hitting his chin on the broken concrete. The gun flew from his hand as he tumbled off of the curb and into the street.

In the next block, the naked girl continued running, not seeing where she was going, just desperately running. She ran until she ran into a barrier, something hard and cold and wet had come up and stopped her forward movement. It was a car.

She stumbled to the side and pulled on the handle, the door was locked. She beat on the window with a sore wrist. The lock popped up. She opened the door and tumbled into the car, dropping as low as possible into the front seat well, becoming as small and invisible as she possibly could.

A loud thump frightened her, fearing she had been found. Percussive noises sounded from somewhere and the car lurched forward. She felt something cloth thrown over her, stiffer than the silk robe, but welcome all the same.

Two blocks away, the big man, still holding the robe and dabbing his chin, came upon his two men, both with their guns out. They were facing a small group of locals, Hispanic and angry. In the middle of the group was a small girl with long, black hair; the Hispanic men were standing around her, also with pistols in their hands.

"We thought it was her," said the cousin.

"And is it?" asked the big man.

"Naw, she's a Mex," said the cousin.

"Then where is she?" asked the big man, looking around behind him.

When the three men had disappeared around the corner, the Hispanics put their guns away and stood around the small girl, to reassure her they wouldn't let anyone take her. The girl's eyes lifted up to her protectors, but not frightened like one might think, but hardened and cold.

"Damn right!" she said, easing the hammer down on her automatic, returning it to the pocket of her coat.

Several blocks away, the car carrying the naked girl pulled into an empty warehouse. For the rest of the night, men in cars and men on foot searched through the warehouse district in the rare L.A. Rain.

The horishi sat in a restaurant in Little Tokyo, drinking too much. Kevin sat in his favorite bar, comforted by his friends. He said he's been dumped by his girlfriend, who had broken up with him after an unexpected arguement. The big man, Rossini, sat in the night club, looking at the yellow robe, stained with dirt and grit from the street. He knew the girl wouldn't be found tonight. The mystery car had scooped her up and had somehow disappeared. When the car reappeared, the girl would there.

Not far away, the naked girl slept in a strange bed after being fed hot soup while the rain fell on Los Angeles.

Getaway Day

It was after eight before Shawn snapped to and realized he was hungry. He'd fed her, now it was time to feed himself. The rain fell steadily, no longer the driving rain of a couple of hours before.

It was Friday, getaway day, and anyone who could get away, did so as early as humanly possible. Fridays, rush hour started around three and went on until after nine. The freeways were still gridlocked with accidents caused by the getaway traffic and zero-visibility rain.

Usually the weather in L.A. was fair and sunny. When the weather got bad, it was the big story on the news.

Shawn roused himself from the chair by the bed and walked to the kitchen.

The weather worked in his favor, he thought. If the rain kept up all weekend and these guys kept roaming the streets, and she has no clothes, she'll want to stay where there's soup and tee shirts—and in his bed; she'll want to keep warm and safe. What they would do on Monday, he hadn't a clue, but until then, Shawn had a beautiful girl in his place—a rare occurrence.

Just to be sure, he went to the window and peeked beneath the heavy drapes. Across the next block, a dim glow traveled down the street, headlights reflected off of the building a block away. They were still looking for the nude girl who disappeared in these streets. Every empty lot would be checked, every dark corner searched, every door tried, every accessible space would be entered and investigated. They wouldn't stop looking for her any time soon.

There was no separate room for the kitchen, just a space set off to the side. Shawn went over and opened a can of beans. After heating it up along with a piece of chicken, it felt like dinner to him. A candlelight dinner for two, chicken soup and chicken & beans. How romantic—even if it sounded better than it was.

He sat down next to the bed to eat, watching her sleep by candlelight while listening to the pummeling rain and bellowing wind. The sound of the freeway a mile away, usually providing a white-noise background, was hidden by the weather.

Finished with dinner, he went downstairs to check the doors. It was a nightly ritual. Carrying a large flashlight, he walked around the big cooler, now dormant and unplugged, and into the back warehouse to the rear doors, large double doors secured with a lock and chains, pegged like the garage door.

As he got near the back, there was a change in the light. He turned off the flashlight. A pool of light passed by the windows, right to left; the sound of a slow car driving by. Someone in the car had a large flashlight and shined it into the windows as they car drove by. Shawn froze and stood behind a support until the lights were gone, then went to check the back doors.

A sound outside made him aware; footsteps. The door shook, making him jump. Someone tested the door from the other side. Whoever it was went to the window and shone a light inside. It was a hooded figure, perhaps the man with the yellow robe over his arm and the gun, who he never wanted to see again.

There was a crash and glass tinkled onto the concrete floor just under the window. The man had broken the window nearest the double-doors. A large arm came through the window and reached to the doors, hoping to find the lock and somehow open it, but it was too far to reach. Whoever designed the building had considered security and made the door lock unreachable.

A dozen different scenarios raced through Shawn's head. He could take his flashlight or a pipe and break the man's arm. But it would alert him of their presence. No, he would run off, only to return with other men, armed men.

He could break the man's arm, then unlatch the door and rush out, striking the man on the head, killing him in the alley. Great, they he'd be a cold-blooded killer with a dead body in the alley. Or, the man could draw his gun and shoot Shawn and the girl with his unbroken arm. No, there were no good outcomes. It was best to cower behind the pillar.

The arm retreated and the man shown the flashlight once more around the interior of the warehouse. He saw only a wide, dark space with a few dusty, broken food carts.

Shawn had left cleaning up the first floor for later on the list. Now he was glad. His workplace was upstairs; he had no interest in the lower level.

Satisfied there was no way in, the hooded stranger moved on. Footsteps faded down the alley and Shawn took a breath, realizing he had not been breathing all the while the stranger was at the window.

The last business to occupy Uncle Mick's warehouse sold large pretzels from rolling carts at fairs and parades. It was only a couple of miles to the Coliseum, where so many games were played and of course, pretzels were sold. Uncle Mick often joked he would get Shawn a job with the pretzel company, a last resort after he failed at everything else. Uncle Mick was glad when Shawn finally found a job he liked. To Shawn, the job was merely tolerable and a money source until his own project got wings.

By the cooler Shawn froze again as a light was shined into the frosted glass on the front door. The door was never used, as the big garage door was Shawn's main entry point. In fact, the front door hadn't been opened since the pretzel company had moved out, leaving three broken carts behind. They sat in the back, gathering dust, sad remnants of a thousand parades and local fairs.

A dark figure stopped at the frosted glass door trying to see inside. Shawn stood in the shadow of the walk-in cooler, hoping prying eyes wouldn't penetrate the darkness to find him. Of course, they couldn't. The frosted glass of the front door was impossible to see through and the iron grate would keep invaders out.

There were two of them outside in front. They turned away and continued down the sidewalk in the rain, talking low as they went. Their shadows could be seen under the garage door, cast by the light across the street. They weren't talking loud enough to be heard, except by each other. When they were gone, Shawn let out a long breath and crept back upstairs in the dark.

He checked the girl again, making sure she still slept. She did. He sat in the soft glow of a single candle and watched the girl sleep.

The clock said 9:45.

"Nine-forty-five on a Friday night and I'm about to nod off. Suffice to say, I am not a party guy!"

Shawn undressed, slipped on a tee shirt and pull-ups and climbed into bed, careful not to disturb his guest. Used to sleeping on his side, he turned, half asleep, and put his arm across the bed, across the slumbering girl. She sighed and stirred, then slept on. So did he.

Outside, the rain fell on the city while sedans with darkened windows and hooded men on foot crisscrossed the neighborhood looking for a bruised and tattooed girl without a stitch on.

Sleep

Listening to the measured breathing of his quiet guest, Shawn reflected on the series of ill-advised decisions and foolish blunders along the way, resulting in his current life situation.

His mother called him Shawn, but spelled it "Sean." His father adopted the current spelling when too many people called him "Seen." Being not good at sports, he tried for academics. He wasn't gifted or even smart, but he understood computers. The new skill set of the 21st Century was perfect.

Aside from living in a warehouse, driving a silver, four-door import that regularly got lost in parking lots, and working in a colorless cubical reminding him of his neighborhood, his new lifestyle had possibilities. He made good money, though more or less entry level—at least with this company. In most other companies, it would be a high-level IT job, but at Tickleme-dot-com, the newest search engine in a world of start-up search engines, just knowing your stuff isn't enough. The level of technical know-how was high, maybe to the bleeding-edge. When he told Uncle Mick he was in Customer Service, Mick remarked it would be good to make a place for himself before they farmed it out overseas.

The workplace yielded no friends. Shawn knew people, but they were work-friends. If not for work, they had nothing to talk about. In the previous few months, there had been over a dozen parties he had heard of taking place without him. He could recall no great embarrassing event, he hadn't insulted anyone, so he assumed they just didn't consider him after-work party material.

It was understandable. After all, he wasn't gay, didn't do drugs, didn't even drink beer. The one time he was invited to a beer after work, the bottle sat in front of him getting warm. When someone noted he wasn't drinking it, Shawn admitted he never drank beer and the cat was out. From then on he was the-guy-who-doesn't-drink-beer.

He thought of Carrie. Carrie was the closest thing he had to a friend at work. She was there the night he announced he didn't drink beer. They were sitting together at the booth watching the show put on by the others from the office. There was Natalie, the busty bombshell from accounting, Larry and Hamid from Customer Service. When Natalie got up to dance, both Larry and Hamid followed after her, panting like Pavlov's pooches.

"Don't you want to go and dance?" asked Carrie.

"Not much for dancing," he replied before realizing it was another nail into his social coffin.

"They're not dancing," Carrie laughed, "just rubbing up against those big boobs. Don't you want to rub up against those big boobs?"

"Never was a fan. I prefer petite to moderate. If I aimed to approach anyone in the office, it wouldn't be Natalie."

"Oh? So who would it be?" inquired Carrie with new-found interested.

"I'd rather not say. There's three reasons why it would be a bad idea."

"Only three?" asked Carrie, now with her full attention on Shawn.

"There might be more, but with three good reasons, there's no need to look for a fourth. After three, any more would be a moot point."

"OK," Carrie allowed. "So what are the three?"

"One," he looked her in the eye for the first time since Natalie left the table. "While there is not a company edict against romantic relationships within the office, there should be, as it's a good idea to avoid same."

"OK," repeated Carrie, unwillingly.

"Secondly, the young lady in question is sufficiently attractive ..."

"Sufficiently attractive?" cut in Carrie.

"I'm stating an issue, not handing out compliments. Sufficiently attractive to have a boyfriend or significant other in the picture. I am not about to rile up a jealous mate. There lies danger."

"OK, so competition is not your strong suit."

"Why look for trouble? Number three: fear of rejection. It's likely the object of my affection will laugh in my face. I don't know if I could take it."

"You think it's likely, do you?"

"It's a possibility," he said, returning his interest to the spectacle on the dance floor.

"Maybe she won't," suggested Carrie.

"But then there's number two – possible boyfriend, perhaps even husband."

"Does she wear a ring?" asked Carrie. Shawn stole a look at her ring finger; Carrie didn't wear a ring.

Carrie was petite-to-moderate and certainly sufficiently attractive, pretty in a girl-next-door way. She might not stack up in Hollywood where bathing beauties from around the country assemble to compete for stardom, but this was downtown, these were real people. In a land where you are what you drive, she was a blue Chevrolet. Shawn had noticed her more than once.

"But then there's number one, dreaded rule number one –

don't drink from the office pool," he reminded her, as well as himself.

"Everyone else does," chided Carrie.

"If everyone else reformatted their hard drive, would you also reformat your hard drive?" He looked at her sideways, making the question rhetorical.

"Point taken. So you're just friends with this person?"

"I hope we're friends."

"Yes, I think you're friends."

"Good. I'm glad." He was.

There was an awkward silence while they watched Larry and Hamid create an embarrassing display on the dance floor with Natalie.

"So, do you want to be friends with benefits?" asked Carrie.

The dance ended and the gruesome trio returned to the table before he could formulate an answer not composed of him saying "Oh! Goodie, goodie!" He did not feel comfortable pushing the concept into bed so he waited.

The office was reorganized before he could execute a plan. Carrie, Larry and Hamid were gone overnight. Natalie was still there. Three new faces took their place. Of the three new hires, one was a guy, one was a lesbian and the other girl was married and pregnant. Shawn reflected it would have been a good idea to have gotten a number for Carrie, but he didn't.

A cold and quiet week followed. Few people spoke with Shawn, who preferred it, without extracurricular interaction with anyone.

When Friday came, he left work at the earliest possible moment, looking forward to the weekend, despite the predicted rain. He didn't know he would have company.

He awoke early Saturday morning. The rain cleaned the accumulated dirt from the skylight high above the center of the loft, where Shawn had placed his bed. The light was dim and gray, but it produced more light than the total dark earlier.

Shawn turned his head to see the girl looking at him, wide awake with big, innocent eyes. She blinked, smiled and shut her eyes again, with a long, deep sigh. Shawn smiled and sighed, closed his eyes and drifted back to sleep.

C. J. Abbot

Suki

It was said the last sleep of the night was the best. Shawn believed it. A restless night was often topped off by deep, relaxing sleep just before he got up.

When he awoke a second time, he felt like he had slept for days. He looked up at the skylight to see the rain still falling. Then he turned his head to see the girl on her left side, her back to him. He the thought it would be a good time to broach the concept of "spoons" to her, but opted instead to lift the cover and inspect her back.

The tattoo was a tree, though more like a vine, with flowers and small leaves which twined from the small of her back, up one side and across her shoulders. There was more, across her hip and down one leg, but it had been merely drawn on and not tattooed as of yet. The main outline and a few leaves and flowers across the shoulders were tattooed on, there for life. The lower part of the tree was sketched in ink and the rest had been washed away in the bath.

Shawn dropped the cover and turned over to slip out of bed. A quick shower and cleanup, then to the series of cubes and baskets passing as a dresser, where he picked out a white pocket-tee and boxer shorts with little Santa Claus figures all over them. Thus prepared for the day, he went to the kitchen to make breakfast.

The coffee had just finished brewing when a small giggle interrupted his labors; standing behind him in bandaged feet, wrapped in the blanket, stood the girl. She giggled, amused at his Santa Claus boxer shorts.

30

Susanne Sukiyama, daughter of a restaurant owner and a bookkeeper, was in her late twenties, but still looked twelve. Thin and small, like her parents, she spent a lot of time proving herself. The cutesy name from her childhood stuck and no matter how hard she tried, she was always "Suki" and not Susanne.

Only her boyfriend and fiancé Kevin seemed to accept her as is, at face value. To him, she was beautifully petite, not just short and small. Kevin had asked her to marry him within a month of their meeting. Plans were going forward and Suki couldn't be happier.

She didn't know her fiancé had developed a love of gambling that ran up a sizable debt. She also didn't know when he wasn't with her, he was with his other friend, Cocaine. Kevin's drug problem made his gambling a problem. The wedding plans were a sham. Suppliers were promising services and goods based on the family name and credit. Even Kevin's family didn't know the extent of his debt. He was headed straight for disaster with no way out. Well, one way out.

To Suki, Kevin was the answer to a prayer. She would now be the wife of a successful businessman, not having to make her way in the world hampered by lack of height and an inability to be taken seriously. To Kevin, she was the answer to a prayer as well: he could trade her for a zero debt balance. After all, they had slept together for several months now and he was getting distracted by other women. The arrangement solved a number of problems for him.

"Mr. Sukiyama?" asked Kevin, peeking his head into the restaurant early on Saturday.

"Kevin! It's good to see you. Is Suki with you?" Mr. Sukiyama had come to grips with the notion of his daughter sleeping with her fiancé. She was not a child anymore, despite her looks. The old values had to be reconsidered in a modern world.

"I thought she was with you. We had our first fight last night and she stormed out. I wanted to apologize." Kevin could lie with the best of them, it was his ace-in-the-hole: if all else fails, lie.

"A fight? What could you two possibly fight about?"

"Oh! Nothing. Hardly anything. Wedding arrangements, who's coming, which cake, silly stuff. She stormed out before I could stop her and she's been out all night."

"She is with a girl friend, crying and eating chocolates. She will come home soon. Have you had breakfast?"

"No. As soon as I woke up, I looked for her. I've called several of her friends, but she's not with the ones I called. I have a few more numbers, but so far, no one's heard anything. I'm getting worried."

"Breakfast will help. Things will look better after a good meal."

Mr. Sukiyama put a hand on Kevin's back and urged him to a table toward the back of the restaurant. Mr. Sukiyama was worried, but he also knew his daughter was headstrong even as a child. She was not one to be pushed around. Still, it was not like her to leave a confrontation; she usually stood her ground. He wondered what the true details were. In relating such an argument, some items are always left out.

Kevin sat waiting for breakfast, trying to look concerned but not overly so. He kept going over in his head the situation as he pretended it to be: Suki argued with him and stormed out of the house, slamming the door behind her. He was afraid the wedding might be off and he would have to mend fences before they could be reunited. She was probably at a girlfriend's, as Mr. Sukiyama had said, eating Rocky Road and talking in disparaging tones about men.

He held this level of concern, putting the true situation out of his mind. Suki had been kidnapped by none other than himself, handed over to modern-day slavers for the sexual delight of businessmen with too much money and twisted appetites. He couldn't think of her situation, which was hopeless. If anyone ever found her again, they wouldn't want her back; she wouldn't last beyond a few years in the life. He would have to wait an appropriate period of time before finding a new girlfriend or thinking about getting married. He also had to suppress the elation he felt at being free of his crushing gambling debts. Suki was lost, and it was a shame, but better her than him. Kevin felt his eyes grow dark, the brows lower at the thought. He forced them to a worried angle, looking sad and hopful for the best outcome.

When breakfast was done he was up immediately.

"I'm going out to look for her. There are places I have forgotten, no doubt."

"Keep me informed, I'm worried. If I find her at my place, I'll call you." Mr. Sukiyama waved a goodbye at the departing Kevin, who tried to keep his concerned look until he was out of sight.

Kevin drove to a friend's place in Agoura, out of the city, high in the rolling foothills north of Los Angeles. There he popped open a beer, sat back on the front porch and opened his phone. He dialed a number and thought about the state of mind he was supposed to be in.

"Hel-lo-o," sang the voice on the other end.

"Melonie? Kevin! Have you seen Suki? Is she with you?"

Out on the small scrap of highway visible in the distance, cars went this way and that, as if looking for Suki. Kevin looked through the contact list on his cell. He had about fourteen more calls before exhausting the list of their friends. By the end of the day, everyone would know how sincere Kevin was in the attempt to find his beloved Suki, who had walked out on him after a few harsh words.

There had been no harsh words, of course. The night before her abduction, Suki had spent the evening looking through bridal magazines. As far as she was concerned, her wedding plans progressed right on schedule: not too fast, not too slow, just as it should be.

Saturday Morning

Saturday morning, Suki woke up and looked at the man sleeping next to her.

Shawn, he said. His name was Shawn. He looked to be in his late 20s, with tousled hair and kind eyes – though they were closed as she watched him sleep.

She was not ready to get up, she was still sleeping, hoping she was safe in her dreams. She watched Shawn as he slept, felt him stir, saw him stretch and roll a quarter turn toward her. She watched his eyes open and look at her. She smiled, closed her eyes and drifted back to sleep, safe in the bed of a stranger.

In her dreams she felt a slight chill as the blanket was pulled away. She tightened her shoulders, remembering the picture drawn on her back, drawn with ink forced into the skin. It wouldn't just go away with time. The blanket returned and she fell into deep sleep once again.

Later, she opened her eyes to find the other side of the bed empty. Shawn was in the kitchen in a tee shirt and boxer shorts. She got up, wrapped herself in the blanket, and walked to the kitchen area, giggling at this spectacle of the man who saved her wearing boxers decorated with Santa Claus figures, making breakfast. She took a step forward, seeking to be close once more to the man who had slept beside her.

To Suki, the man she loved had betrayed her, sold her into slavery to be used as a sex toy, while a total stranger had saved her, taken her in and bandaged her feet. He had slept by her without violating her. How often does that happen? He was a rare find, to be sure. She could fall in love with this man. If only she could stay here forever, inside this cave of wood, far from the scene of her worst day, and never have to face the world outside again.

She looked at the boxer shorts again and giggled. Shawn turned and smiled.

"Yes," thought Suki, "I could fall in love with this man and stay here with him forever."

"Good morning." Shawn looked at the smiling girl, looked down at his shorts, then back to the girl. He felt silly wearing Santa boxers out of season, but he was ready with a come-back.

"It's 'National Wear-What's-Clean Day.' I observe it religiously."

The girl giggled. She pulled the blanket closer around her and blushed.

"Thank you," she whispered. Her voice was still strained and hoarse. "Thank you for saving me."

"You're welcome. Sit at the table, I'll pour you some coffee, then we'll have pancakes."

"Again, I thank you."

"I'm Shawn, Shawn Cauver."

"I remember." She pulled a chair out and sat at the table, pulling her legs and feet beneath her, making a cocoon of the blanket.

"What's your name?" Shawn asked, pouring two cups of coffee, placing one in front of the girl. He indicated the sweetener and non-dairy creamer on the table.

"Suki," said the girl, tasting the coffee black. "This is good," she said, holding the cup with both hands, as if to keep them warm.

"Suki, cute."

"Suzanne Sukiyama."

"So you're Japanese?" Shawn asked.

"Yes, uh, but born here."

"Hm!" Shawn said, paying attention to his collection of pancake supplies. He wanted to say much more, but 'Hm!' seemed appropriate.

"Genetic," she commented. She meant her size, like a twelve-year-old.

Shawn figured she spent a lot of time explaining it to people and had boiled it down to one word to save time. He changed the subject.

"What's the tattoo all about? I mean, given the opportunity, I would take you as you are, without further adornment or enhancement."

"Those men are criminals."

"The guns gave it away."

Suki sat looking at the table while Shawn mixed the batter in a bowl. By the time the tap-tap-tap of the wooden spoon on the side of the bowl subsided, she had put the pieces together.

"My – my fiancé had a money problem, I guess. As near as I can figure, I was traded to pay his debt."

Suki sipped the coffee, fortifying herself.

"It's unthinkable!" she whimpered.

Shawn reached over to the work desk, picking up the box of tissue and placing it on the dining table. Suki took a tissue, with a small nod to him. He continued mixing, though the batter was already just right. Suki sighed.

"They said I might have," Suki shuddered, took in a breath and continued. "five or six good years left before men would no longer want me. With a body-tattoo, I would look like a girl brought here for prostitution."

"Here? Not in Japan?"

"In Japan, they like American girls. In America, Japanese girls. Irezumi, traditional tattoo, makes me Japanese. A

Horishi, a traditional artist, was found." Suki lowered her eyes, looking at her hands. "They talk about these things in soft voices. They say few girls ever get out of the life."

Shawn looked at her with a knot in his throat. This was more serious than he thought. The girl was in big trouble and he was not sure of what to do next.

"Then we'll just have to make sure they don't get their hands on you," he said in a cracked and strained voice.

Suki reached out a small hand and touched him on the side. Shawn smiled and returned to the stove. He poured batter into the pan and stood watching them with a flipper in his hand.

"You'll stay with me for now. Maybe we can smuggle you out to a friend's place or somewhere you'll be safe. What if we go to the police?"

"And say what? We have no proof. By the time they find and break into the place where they held me, it would be cleaned out – or burned to the ground."

He wanted to suggest the FBI, but the same thing would apply, without hard evidence, she could be a drunken night gone wrong. The boyfriend could say anything and it would be a "his-word/her-word" thing.

"I can disappear," said Suki, considering for the first time something which would have shocked her yesterday.

"As far as I'm concerned, you have. You live here now. I'll take care of you." Shawn felt more for her than her boyfriend did; he would never sell her into slavery.

Shawn brought pancakes, three to a plate, to the table along with a small bottle of syrup. They ate in silence.

There was not much to be said. The situation was a terrible one, with betrayal and evil intent abounding. Their position was precarious and the future looked bleak, but they had pancakes and coffee. Shawn clearly cared about her, the girl he found in the rain, and Suki felt safe for the first time since the nightmare began.

"Thank you," she said again.

"You said."

"I know."

"You're welcome."

Cochran

"I'm surrounded by idiots!" muttered Harlan Cochran to his bagel and cream cheese. He sat on the patio facing the rolling Hollywood Hills. Behind him, the mansion supposed to belong to someone famous, he couldn't remember who – it didn't matter. Today, little mattered. He had lost an easy deal. He hated losing an easy deal.

It was so simple. The man had lost – lost big. So he owed on his gambling debts, owed on his recreational drugs – four hundred thousand dollars to date. One cute Japanese sex goddess, decorated with something aesthetic, would pay it back in less than a year. Anything after a year would be pure gravy. The imbeciles at the club had blown it. They let the girl get through a back window and out into the world, half drawn and half naked.

He raised a finger. The man on his left in black slacks and pressed white shirt stepped forward. Cochran held up a hand.

"Not you," he said without turning his head. "You." He pointed to the other man, in the black suit, black shirt and black tie. The man stepped forward, looking sheepish, given his sinister presentation.

"Yes, Mr. Cochran."

"The boy's still on the hook for the outstanding."

"Of course. Yes sir. I'll see to it." The man took a step back.

Stu Coleman knew it wasn't his fault. He was not even there. It was stupid Rossini's fault, him and his two dimwit cousins. Give them one lousy club to run and they think they're world-class hoods, yet they can't keep their paws on one tiny girl.

Cochran finished his bagel and sat back, looking at the houses dotting the Hollywood Hills. He didn't mind the money. Four hundred grand was chicken-feed in the overall picture. There was reputation to be considered. If he let this fish off the hook, debts will be dropping all over town like last night's rain.

This was a unique situation. The boy had a girlfriend who was mature but looked like a child, and Asian. She could be kept wrapped in a narcotic haze, decorated like a Japanese sex toy and could work for years. The debt would be paid back many times over. American businessmen would pay for the fantasy of an underage Asian girl. By the time her beauty had begun to fade, her family and friends would have forgotten all about her. She would be a nobody. Nobodies could disappear without questions asked.

But the girl vanished into a hard and unyielding city. She had to have help. But who would help her? They must know they are buying a death sentence, the inevitable payback for prolonging the search. Rossini and his cousins were a waste of time. A bad bet. He had put his faith in the wrong people – again.

The demand for young, Asian girls among his American clientele grew more taxing on his resources. His Tokyo connection delivered to a point, but girls were getting lost along the way. Two brothers named McQueen had been in charge of the transfer. They botched it and the girls got away. The McQueen brothers were buried in the Nevada desert. He had to turn to Rossini and his cousins to handle this deal. It was a bad choice. He never thought he would miss the McQueen boys.

"Coleman!" he spat, not turning his head.

"Yes, sir," Coleman took a step closer.

41

"We'll need a couple of more men. Reach out, find someone who can be trusted and bring them in. What our team lacks in brains we'll make up in numbers."

"I'll find them, Mr. Cochran." Coleman stepped back to his original position. Now he had two errands. Neither one was difficult. He couldn't screw this up, he was sure. The boss was not in a forgiving mood.

"Now!" spat Cochran over his shoulder.

"Yes, sir," said Coleman, turning to go inside at the fastest possible pace. At his car, he pulled out his phone, hoping the signal would be strong.

"Walker?" Coleman said into the phone. "You still got a guy who wants to work? You vouch for him, right? OK, I need you both. Come out to the house today, right away. Come equipped; come dressed – ready to work. OK. See you then."

Coleman slid the phone shut, certain he had filled the need. Now to find the kid!

He knew Kevin wasn't a kid, but he was as dumb as a kid, so he was "the kid." He had laid down all his money and lost it. Then he laid down his girlfriend and lost her. Now he was still in the red column and didn't even know it. The kid was about to have a bad day.

An hour later, Walker arrived with another man, both in dark gray suits.

"Surroyan," said Walker to Coleman.

"Surroyan, just do what Walker says and don't hesitate."

"No problem," said Surroyan.

Coleman noted the fullness of the coat, a style allowing room for a holstered pistol. If it had not been a push-come-to-shove day, he would have done a more in-depth interview, but there was more nearly half-a-million dollars at stake, a girl in the wind and a boyfriend to locate and educate. Coleman turned his attention to Walker. He handed the man a thin folder.

"Big doings right off the bat. Here's the 411 on a guy we need to find, you sit on his place. If he shows up, bring him here. I need to deliver some info of my own."

"No problem," said Walker. He turned to Surroyan and chucked him on the arm, tossing his head toward the car out front. The two men left with the folder.

Coleman smiled, impressed with how fast he had handled both tasks, and at the same time. In his head it was a done deal. He had handed off to Walker, who he knew. Walker vouched for Surroyan. Together they'd bring in the kid. Who knows, maybe the kid had another Asian girlfriend he could hand over.

First Aid

After breakfast, Shawn spent an hour dabbing antibiotic ointment on Suki's back. The tattooing was clearly not finished, but the completed part was beautiful. The artist clearly knew his art. He looked beneath the leaves and flowers at the shape of Suki's back. She was more beautiful; no piece of art in the world could enhance her beauty. He wondered at the thought process of anyone who believed such loveliness could be enhanced. He helped her into a clean oversize shirt then slipped the robe over her. She sighed as she settled in under the covers.

Lifting the bottom of the cover, Shawn attended to her feet, still bruised and cut from her run through the rain the evening before.

The rain fell on the skylight above and could be heard hitting the roof. On a day like this, Shawn wouldn't have gone out anyway. There wasn't anything he needed, no one to see, nothing outside mattered. It was as if his whole world was what he held in his hands, the small feet of this stranger who had come into his life alone and afraid, chased by armed men.

He put a pair of clean, white socks on her feet and pulled the cover over them. Suki sighed and stirred, her eyes closed. The patter of the rain on the skylight, the tap-tap-tap on the roof, mesmerized her to sleep.

Shawn remembered the boat trip his family had taken when he was just a boy. He slept through most of it, rocking to the rhythm of the vessel, letting it lull him to sleep. Suki needed sleep. The loft was her vessel. He would ensure the waves didn't get too rough.

Shawn stretched out beside her and looked at the girl as she breathed in and out. He closed his eyes as well, pulling the cover over him. He pulled his body next to hers and sighed. He was aware of the rain on the skylight overhead, pattering across the roof and running down the broken gutter out back to the alley. Without lights, without noises coming from the warehouse, the searchers would continue walking and driving past without stopping.

He drifted off, still listening, reassuring himself the rain was the only sound he heard, nothing to interfere with Suki's sleep – or his own.

He awoke an hour later still listening to the rain, watching the shadows, with a protective arm around Suki.

Shawn became aware of his arm and the hand at the end of it. He held a breast, a small, warm breast with a hard nipple. He gave a quiet gasp and released Suki's breast. He pulled his arm back, slowly, so as not to wake her – but he felt a hand on his as Suki guided his back to her breast.

"No, It's OK," she whispered.

They lay there for another half hour, until the rain stopped and hunger once again became a priority. Shawn got up and went to the kitchen.

"What would you be doing if it weren't for me?" asked Suki.

She sat up in bed while Shawn put a meal together. He stood at the kitchen counter in a pair of old cotton pull-ons and a tee shirt. Lunch was chicken soup, something warm for a cold, rainy day.

"Working on my guitar project," answer Shawn without looking away from the stove.

"Then you should work on your guitar project. I'd rather watch you than have you watch me all day long."

Shawn turned to her, a concerned look on his face. Then he turned back to the task at hand. Stirring the soup in the

45

pan with a wooden spoon settled his thoughts and put them in order.

"Then I'll show you what I'm doing and you'll get better faster."

Suki smiled and watched Shawn pour soup into two bowls and place them on the table. She had never seen a man do this before. She watched him all through the short meal.

After eating, Shawn washed the bowls and put them away. Suki was impressed.

"Why don't you just leave them until later?" she asked.

"This building is prone to bugs. If I left these dishes out, we'd have company in no time. They're harder to get rid of than to prevent."

Suki looked at him with her head askew, like a small puppy seeing something for the first time. Here was a man who thought things out, one who was not afraid to wash a bowl, one who was mindful of where he lived.

Shawn carried her to a seat next to the workbench in the corner. He checked the heavy curtains to ensure no light would pass through and turned on the work light. A mass of wires and electronic pieces covered the work table. On wooden blocks sat an old guitar, a Fender Stratocaster which had clearly seen better days. Shawn sat on an ergonomic chair, on his knees with his legs tucked under. He indicated the parts as he spoke.

"The pickups here take the vibration of the strings and turn it into a wireless signal going to the amplifier here." He indicated a small laptop, open but not yet switched on. "The signal is sent to these speakers – loud, of good quality and all wireless. It will revolutionize the industry. The guitarist will walk into a gig with an ax in one hand and a suitcase in the other. It's all he needs. No amp, no wires, no leads. He can walk anywhere around the room and this will pick up the signal."

"Where are the speakers?" asked Suki.

"Here," said Shawn, indicating two small, black cubes the size of his palm.

"But the speakers are so small," said Suki, surprised.

"Yes, but powerful enough to fill a medium-sized night club. Add two more at the back and you have a large room covered. All I need is..." Shawn drifted off, looking up at the picture tacked to the support beam to his left, a picture of a tall, thin column on a round base.

"What is that?" asked Suki.

"The bass column, what I'm saving for next."

"So this is all to play guitar music?"

"Yes, if only I could get it to work."

"Mmmm," agreed Suki.

Surroyan

Walker drove the black Suburban like a grandmother. When the crew tinted the windows, he stood watching them with his suit jacket open – they all knew he was armed. He wanted to make sure it was perfect. Even now, he carried a damp towel under the seat, ready to wipe off bird droppings before they dry. Surroyan smiled at how Walker micromanaged the vehicle.

Everyone called him Surroyan, even his closest friends, though he wasn't quite sure who they were right now, as it had been so long since he had seen them. He had spent the last year and a half getting on Walker's good side. Jobs in this business were around, but with highly placed people the air got thinner the higher up you went.

Surroyan had a gun under his coat, just like Walker. The difference was, Surroyan was skilled. He went to the range several times a week, took his weapon seriously. He could hear a noise, turn, find the target and put a slug in it in a heartbeat. Surroyan was good.

He was also a loner – typical of the best of his breed. He had no wife, no kids, no girlfriend and no regular drinking buddies. In fact, he didn't drink. Nor did he take drugs or lay down with hookers. As a result, he lacked weaknesses to be exploited. Surroyan was a pro.

Now he had an assignment from Cochran. Even though Walker was the primary on this job, it wouldn't stay that way. Walker was too careful in the car and too reckless out of it. He was 40% screw-up. Like 40% chance of showers, if it rains, you're wet. When Walker screwed up, he would be 100% in trouble. Sooner or later, Sorroyan knew he would be taking assignments direct from Cochran and telling Walker to come along. He would also drive better than Walker.

"So we just bring this guy Kevin in once we find him?" asked Surroyan.

"Yep! Bring him in; Coleman wants to talk with him," said Walker.

"We know what he's done?"

"Doesn't matter. We do what we're told. Coleman knows what he's doing."

"I was just curious," said Surroyan.

"Yeah, you know what that'll get you."

Apparently this was one of those jobs you didn't discuss. Surroyan didn't speak for the rest of the ride. He was smart enough to know when silence was golden.

Kevin's place was typical for the Hollywood Hills, the entrance was on the third floor and the rest of the house hung off of the side of the mountain. There was no response at the door. A glance inside the garage showed it was empty; Kevin's car was gone. In a town where you drive everywhere. He was out. Walker parked up the block facing the house, as far away as he could get without rounding a corner. If and when Kevin came back, they'd be there waiting for him.

"Are we the only one's on this guy? Seems like a thin thread," said Surroyan.

"Rossini and his guys lost the girl, so I don't think they'll have anything else on their agenda but finding her. Cochran has two guys with him at all times at the house, but there's the McQueen brothers – Oh, wait, no – I was wrong, the McQueen brothers aren't around anymore."

Walker grinned at Surroyan, like there was a joke they shared. Surroyan didn't get it, but didn't push it either.

"OK! One question: What girl?" asked Surroyan.

"This guy owed. He had a girl. So Cochran took the girl. She'll turn tricks until the debt's paid. Thing is, the girl ran away. So she might come back here, or else he'll hide her. I don't know. Something will happen and the guy will be in on it. When it does, we grab him. We grab the guy, we get the girl back, Cochran is happy, we get paid. End of story."

"Yeah," said Surroyan, "end of story."

Old Friends

"Mike?" Shawn said into the phone.

"Uh, hi, this is Mike, leave a message when you hear the tone."

"Mike, stop it. This is Shawn. I need to talk to you."

"OK, OK, just a minute."

Shawn heard fumbling about and soft swearing as Mike prepared for doing anything requiring being awake. He was the sort who would play music until dawn, sleep until dark and say the day was already shot, so he might as well go out and play some more. Shawn knew of no more talented a waste of time in LA than Mike.

"OK, what?" said a sleepy voice.

"It's Shawn."

"Hey, Shawn. How's it hangin' man? You still doin' – uh – whatever you were doin'? What were you doin', anyway?"

"A job, but it's not important."

"Uh, yeah! You got that right," chuckled sleepy Mike.

"Listen, you said something about Joyce. You remember Joyce? The singer who had the mark she would paint on her cheek? You went with her a long time, didn't you?"

"Man, ancient history, and kinda painful. You know how to hurt a guy! Yeah, Joyce got a gig in Asia and went big-time – never spoke to us low-life's again."

"Yeah, tell me about it. Where did she go?"

"Gig was in Japan – front vocalist for a band – they love those leggy Black chicks. She said if it didn't work out she'd

51

come back, but I never heard from her again and neither did anyone else."

A shudder went through Shawn. Suki had awakened a fear in him: he was not prepared for the realities of life.

"So, what? Did she marry some rich guy or become a star?" Or, he added in his head, did she become a sex slave and meet a horrible end.

"I don't know," said Mike, who thought he had already answered the question. "All I know is my number hasn't changed and I never heard from her again. So, what's up? You got a gig, or an itch you can't scratch or what?"

"No, nothing. I just thought about old friends. We should get together for music and a brew one night."

"Yeah, OK. Let me know when and I'll be there."

"You got any gigs coming up?"

"Naw! Nothing sure, just a lot of impromptu jams. If I get anything, I'll let you know."

"I might have something for you soon regarding your next guitar."

"You still messin' with your old Strat? You'll never get the thing to work."

"Oh, ye of little faith! You hide and watch. The world is going wireless and so am I. Soon you'll be setting up less than twelve ounces of equipment for a gig. You'll be laughing out the other side when you have to buy it retail. Take care."

"Yeah, man. Keep the faith."

Joyce and Mike were an item. When she left for Japan, he was crushed. She was chasing a star: lead singer in a packaged band destined for great things. They all assumed she lived the life of a mega-star, no time for the little people of her past. But now Shawn had the feeling her talent was wasted while she lived the life of forced prostitution, drugged to keep her compliant. The thought made him cold. When he turned around, Suki stood looking at him, concerned.

"We're going to have to go to the police, or the FBI – someone," said Shawn.

"Do you think anyone would listen?"

"They have to listen. We'll show them your back and bring them down here to see who's searching the streets with guns. We'll show them your feet as a convincer."

Shawn put her in a second pair of socks, pull-up bottoms pinned at the waist and a tee shirt a size too small for him. Suki swam in his clothes and looked like a ragamuffin. Still, purpose put style aside and she got into the car without protest or second thought. She looked like a bundle of laundry in the front seat.

Shawn looked out of the glass in the door, first to one side, then to the other. No one could be seen, no one was looking, no one chasing them now. He motioned Suki to slide down in the seat and opened the garage door. After pulling the Toyota out, he closed the door and looked both ways again, just to make sure. There was no one in sight.

Shawn smiled as he got into the drivers' seat and put the car in gear.

C. J. Abbot

Les Girls

Leaving the warehouse was not a problem, escaping the warehouse district proved to be difficult though. Shawn had turned two corners when he saw the black Lexus patrolling the neighborhood.

They must have been looking for a small dark Toyota because the Lexus pulled in front of them and three men jumped out of the car. Shawn slammed the Toyota into reverse, pulled back around and into a small alley, just enough to have a clear path to the street away from the black Lexus. But the men from the car didn't jump in to give chase, they pulled guns.

As Shawn stepped on the gas, a flurry of bullets peppered the car, bursting the front tires and sending the car into the fence on the far side of the street.

Shawn looked at Suki, her eyes wide as she was pulled from the passenger seat by a large man in a black suit. He held a gun to her head. Shawn was pulled out of the driver's side by the other two men.

"Blow his head off!" shouted the large man in the black suit. The other two grinned and looked at each other with greedy looks. They lived for this.

"Not here, idiots! Someone might see. Take him off into the alley."

The two wanna-be wiseguys nodded, as if it had just occurred to them as a good idea. One grabbed Shawns arm and swung him around in the direction of the alley. The second guy shoved him hard and Shawn stumbled forward.

54

For Shawn, each detail came into focus – the overflowing dumpster, the bent bicycle wheel, the cracked wooden pallet against the wall, the smell of rotting food, the rough, uneven bricks beneath him.

Shawn knew he had to do something. He righted himself, stamped down hard on the instep of the closest guy. Letting out a yell and hopping on one foot, the injured hit-man stumbled into his accomplice knocking him into the wall, his pistol clattering to the brickwork. He let out a cry as his head hit the side of the building and he slumped to the ground. Shawn pulled the pistol from the first man's belt and shot him in the leg. The man screamed and grabbed his leg, the blood gushing through his fingers. Shawn picked up the fallen pistol and turned to the second man getting up off the ground. Shawn shot him in the leg as well. It worked once; he figured it would work again. It did.

Shawn left them and ran from the alley into the street, toward the black Lexus and the big man in the black suit who held Suki, screaming and kicking. Shawn raised both pistols and fired at him. With Suki so small and the man so large, he had no fear of missing her. He didn't expect to miss him as well, however.

Both bullets flew by the man's head, but it got his attention. He let go of Suki and pulled a pistol from his shoulder holster. As he raised the gun, taking experienced aim at Shawn, Suki flew into action. She shot up, raising her fist into the man's crotch, making him double over. His face turned blue and his eyes bulged. She dealt him a round-house kick sending him flying back into the car and then to the concrete on his back. Suki jumped up and landed on top of the man, elbow first, forcing the air from his lungs. She picked up the pistol from the ground and shot him in the calf. The man reached for his leg with his left hand, but couldn't get to it for the bulk in between.

"Get in!" yelled Shawn, running toward them. Suki slid across the seat of the Lexus with Shawn close behind her. He put the car in gear and left the bleeding men in the street not far from his poor Toyota, crashed into the storm fencing and full of bullet holes.

Shawn needed an escape route, a straight line between two points. He hit the gas heading for Alameda Boulevard, into the flow of traffic.

As he left the neighborhood, he passed the club on the corner, "Les Girls, Girls, Girls." Suki slumped in the seat. Shawn took in a breath to speak, to ask what was up. His thought was interrupted by two police cars heading straight for him, sirens blaring, red and blue lights swirling.

Shawn put his blinker on, old habits kicking in, and pulled around the corner, being overly safe, onto Alameda as the police cars swerved into the warehouse district. The police cars flew by him on the way to the location of the "shots fired" reports.

"Now where?" asked Suki, her voice weak and trembling.

"The one place they won't look for us." He opened the glove compartment and took out a leather folder. "Find the registration."

"We're going to his place?" asked Suki disbelieving.

"Well, we've got the keys. We don't have the keys to my place, they're still in my car."

The picture was clear to both of them: Shawn's Toyota was now part of a crime scene, his keys dangling from the ignition. The only keys Shawn and Suki had were in the ignition of the Lexus, they fit the address on the registration, a hillside house in the Silver Lake area. Shawn punched the gas, headed toward Riverside Drive, along the tracks to Silver Lake.

"Carlo Rossini," said Suki. "He was one of the men who gave me to the tattoo artist, just after Kevin..." She remembered her fiancé, the one who sold her out to international sex slavers. "Kevin!" she repeated, low and slow, her eyes dark and narrow.

"What about him?" asked Shawn.

"We could go to Kevin's house." Suki looked at the pistol she'd put on the floor of the Lexus when she got in, planning to use it to have a chat with Kevin.

"I don't think it's a good idea. We'll let the police deal with him."

She knew it was a better idea, but not the one she liked at the moment.

"Maybe Rossini's got a girlfriend," said Suki, looking down at her put together outfit. One of the pins had come lose and she tried to tie the waist of the pullups into a knot. It wasn't working.

"Who?" asked Shawn.

"Carlo Rossini, of course, the man whose car we have just stolen after shooting him, the man whose house we are about to invade."

"I didn't shoot him, you shot him."

"Yes, well, you shot his two friends, in the legs."

"It seemed like a good way to keep them busy."

"I know, I got the idea from you."

"You shot him in the calf," noted Shawn, getting into the game of it.

"Well, he could reach his thigh. He's too big to reach his calf. He won't be able to bend down to put his hand on it to stop the bleeding."

"The police will have fun with them," said Shawn. The men sported holsters and extra bullets, but no guns, so it would appear they were shot with their own guns and therefore,

Shawn shot in self-defense. The police might realize whoever turned the corner were the people who shot them. They'll have his car and his registration. They'll have an all-points-bulletin out on him in no time. The police will be-on-the-look-out. But the one place they won't think to look is the home of Carlo Rossini.

The garage door was huge! It covered a double garage with one open space and one space filled with a vintage Pontiac GTO, a baby-blue convertible. The house itself was built into the side of a hill, overlooking a valley littered with similar homes built into the sides of hills.

Carlo Rossini was a bachelor but clearly had girls in. A collection of ladies' clothing hung in each of the three bedrooms. Suki chose a short robe of silk with a sash over a short tank-top and pajama-bottom pants. There was a pair of cloth shoes they fit if she wore them over Shawn's socks. She still looked a mess, but she felt better about it.

"Have you looked at yourself?" asked Suki, walking into the kitchen. Shawn looked for something to pass for a late lunch.

"No, what do I look like?"

"You're covered in blood spatter!"

Shawn turned and looked into the mirror in the entry hall. His shirt was torn and covered in blood splotches from two directions. Both of the men he shot had left their blood on him, as well as having torn his shirt as he pulled away from them. He left off the idea of a late lunch in favor of a clean shirt.

Rossini was a large man and his shirt was two sizes too big for Shawn. He rolled the sleeves and left the tail out, blousing like a tent around a pole. He looked ridiculous, but at least it wasn't covered with blood. He wrapped his own shirt in a plastic bag and put it in the trash bin by the garage.

"Now what?" asked Suki. She sat on the sofa, looking at the wide empty space in the middle of the coffee table.

"We can't go back to the warehouse, not yet. It's in my uncle's name, but they might find out I live there. It's not unheard of. And there's more guys looking for us than those three, you can be sure."

"Then we can't stay here forever either."

"No, Rossini is bound to come back sooner or later."

Suki got up, sinking into the chair next to him, putting her head on his chest.

"Hold me, Shawn."

"I've got you," he said. He put a hand on her head, smoothing her hair. It felt good – for both of them.

Shots Fired

The police poured in from all sides, into the empty streets of the warehouse district where the reports of *Shots Fired* drew them. The aging Toyota was full of holes, both front tires blown and it had plowed into the storm fencing surrounding the empty lot on the corner.

A large man in a suit lay in the middle of the street. He screamed, reaching for his lower leg, trying in vain to get over his large mid-section to get a hand on the bleeding wound. He had just recovered his breath, gasping, his face going from blue to exasperated red. He was sore from blows to the groin and to the face, with a growing bruise on his chin.

"Got two more over here!" yelled an officer from the alley.

Sergeant Wentworth turned his head toward the alley. Sure enough, two men lay on the raw brick, agonizing with wounds in their thigh muscles. One man's wound looked as if it might have hit a bone. The other man's wound was on the inside thigh, in the fatty part and high, near the crotch. He had the look of someone who had just escaped disaster.

"Any weapons?" yelled Wentworth to the officer in the alley. The officer looked around.

"Nope! Nothing here."

"Or here," yelled an officer standing next to the big man in the street. "Got a holster, extra clip, but no weapon."

"Call it in, get a wagon for these guys. Let's see if we can find out what the hell's going on here." Sergeant Wentworth walked over to the big man on the concrete. "Name?" he asked.

"Jesus! Call an ambulance! I've been shot! Stop the blood, will ya?"

"Name?" repeated Wentworth, "And don't say 'Jesus' again, you wouldn't pass as Hispanic."

"Hey! I'm bleedin' here!" screamed the big man.

"Ambulance is on the way, but you're not going anywhere until I get some answers." Wentworth directed a communication to the officer standing by. "Get his wallet."

The officer opened the man's coat and pulled out his wallet.

"Carlo Rossini. There's a business card here, 'Les Girls, Girls, Girls.' It's right up the street, we passed it just at Alameda."

"What happened here, Mr. Rossini?" Wentworth asked.

"A car-jacking! What do you think? A guy and a chick, they shot me and took my car, a Lexus sedan, black, brand new."

"So let me see if I've got this," said Wentworth. "A guy and his chick pulled you and your associates from your car, disarmed you, shot you and then riddled their car with bullets before fleeing in your Lexus. Have I got it right?"

He would have smiled at the thought of it, but Sergeant Malcolm Wentworth never smiled – never.

"Yeah, you got it right," said Rossini. "Now, how about that ambulance?"

As if in response, the sound of a siren was heard in the distance. As it grew in volume, Wentworth walked over to the alley. He waved an officer to the Toyota. The officer nodded and strode toward the wrecked vehicle.

"Hear that sound?" asked Wentworth to the two wounded men. He crouched down so as to be near to them and spoke softly, a tone he had practiced for years for striking terror in the hearts of criminals.

C. J. Abbot

"That's the sound of salvation. But before they take you away to the land of nice, clean hospital rooms and pain killers, you're gonna to tell me what happened here."

The two men looked at each other, as if communicating telepathically, asking permission to spill the story and thus get needed medical attention. Wentworth looked at their belts. Each had an empty holster. No weapon was found. Either the assailant had thrown the guns where they could not be seen or he still had them. Wentworth wondered if the man and girl could be considered armed and dangerous.

The two men looked at Wentworth, not knowing quite what to say. Any way they tried it out, they couldn't make it come out with them in the right. They needed someone to tell them what to say.

"I want a lawyer," said one man. "And a doctor – I'm shot, and my goddamn foot's broken."

Wentworth smirked and turned to the other man.

"Yeah, me too. Except my foot's not broken, but the other thing. Yeah."

Wentworth shook his head. A shell casing caught his attention. It was a nine millimeter, copper. Another was close to it, only steel. The casings were from different pistols.

"Collect these," he told the officer, pointing at the two shells. He got up and walked toward the wrecked Toyota. The officer in the alley collected the two shells, placing them in different envelopes. He wrote on the envelopes and put them in his pocket.

The officer standing by the Toyota had the registration in his hand.

"Shawn Cauver. Says here he lives in Los Angeles. Nothing in it, no weapons, nothing of interest. Bullets came from outside, none from the inside. Keys still in the ignition. There's traces of blood on the passenger side seat and floor."

"Call a tow, I want this brought in. Put out an APB for a black Lexus, get the plate from DMV, belonging to one Carlo Rossini."

The officer nodded and went to the radio car.

"Now, why were those two in the alley?" Wentworth asked himself, in the same soft voice. He looked from the alley to Rossini, still on the ground, swearing and trying to recover from attacks on multiple levels.

"What do you think?" asked the officer standing over Rossini.

"I think Shawn Cauver and his girl are glad to be alive right now. I think when we find the black Lexus, there's going to be an interesting story."

Wentworth thought about the shell casings found at the scene. "One, two," he counted, "and one by Rossini. Nine-mil in the alley. Rossini was shot with a different pistol, his own pistol, a .38. These guys too. They were all shot with their own pistols, looks like."

Wentworth turned to the officer on is right.

"I want these all logged separately, and check Rossini for other wounds and injuries; I want a complete list. Test all of these guys for gunshot residue. If they test positive, I want them charged – just enough to keep them until we find out what the hell happened here. There were reports of gunshots last night as well, but nothing found. These are connected, I'm sure of it."

Paramedics ran from downed man to downed man, yelling statistics and conditions, calling for items from the truck and doing what they could for the wounded gunmen. Officers typed on dashboard computers and radioed in orders. In the center of the activity stood Sergeant Wentworth, his mouth twisted, one eye squinted, trying to put the pieces together.

C. J. Abbot

Little GTO

"We can't stay here," said Shawn.

He stood in the doorway to the kitchen, lost in the shirt, two sizes too large for him. His eyes didn't focus on anything in particular; he was preoccupied.

"Why not?" asked Suki. She shifted on the couch, uncomfortable in any clothing now. Her back itched and ached alternately. She felt the world closing in. She could be abducted or killed depending on the whim of the men who drove sedans and carried guns.

"Because the police were already on the scene as we were leaving. By now they have the guy's name and description of the car. Figures they'll look here. No matter what, someone will come here sooner or later."

"Oh, I didn't think," said Suki, getting up.

"It just occurred to me."

Shawn went to the garage. He looked at the Lexus, sitting there, with two bullet holes in the roof just above the door. He nodded in agreement to his own realization: a car with a couple of bullet holes looks suspicious. He eyes took in the GTO parked next to the Lexus.

The little blue GTO had the top up. The key hung on one of the hooks next to the door to the house. He took the key and called to Suki. He held the house door open as she looked out. Shawn's smile said he had found a solution. Suki looked at the GTO and at Shawn in disbelief.

"It might get some attention, but it won't get the kind of attention a bullet-ridden mob-car would get," said Shawn.

Suki sighed hard, getting used to doing things both strange and uncomfortable. She walked down the three steps to the garage and the waiting GTO. She looked into the window, pulled at the handle and turned to Shawn.

"Where are we going?" she asked as she got in.

"The police," said Shawn, getting in. Suki bit her lip. She wasn't ready for the police.

Shawn pulled the GTO out of the garage and aimed it toward the driveway. His worst fears were immediately realized as a black Cadillac sedan pulled in front of him, blocking his escape. Two men in suits opened the front doors of the sedan. Shawn saw guns and knew he had nowhere to go. Something inside snapped.

"Run!" he yelled to Suki.

Suki leapt out and ran back up the short driveway, looking for a place to escape, but there was none – the yard was closed off. She turned toward the back of the house but was caught by a huge arm. Suki screamed as she was pulled off of the ground with one mighty swoop. She twisted her body, brought up her leg and kicked hard at the face just a few inches above her. Her heel caught the man's jaw and he fell back with a cry loosening his grip on her. Suki rolled out of his arm and started across the yard, not knowing what she would do once she got to the fence at the end. The second man tackled her around the legs and she hit the grass with a thump.

Shawn got out of the car and stood by the running GTO. An older man, holding a shiny automatic pistol got out of the back seat of the Cadillac blocking his escape. He faced Shawn and smiled, his eye fixed on the pocket of the shirt hanging around Shawn like a tent.

"CTR, Rossini's monogram. You know, when I heard he was collected and his car gone, I figured you might come here, and here you are – in Rossini's shirt. You take the cake!"

Suki's high-pitch shriek followed by the man's howl of pain made both Shawn and the man with the pistol turn. Running feet and the sound of a body hitting the ground followed. Shawn turned back to see the man by the car raise his gun and aim it at him. Shawn ran several steps down the street and dove behind a parked car. Seeing the bushes in front of the next house, he leaped into the yard.

The two men came out holding a kicking Suki with some difficulty. They looked at the man by the car and then to Shawn. For a moment, they didn't know whether to hold on to the girl or drop her and shoot the guy.

"Forget about it! I got him!" the man yelled He fired several shots. Shawn ran, dodging bullets close enough to feel, making the loose shirt billow around him.

Suki cried out. Shawn turned to see her being carried screaming into the car.

Shawn crumpled to the ground as the bullet flew just above his head. He rolled onto the grass, up to his feet and around the next house as two more bullets sped by in quick succession.

Car doors slammed, tires screeched and the Cadillac disappeared into the distance. Shawn looked around as the blood drained from his face; Suki was gone.

Welcome Back

"Welcome back, my dear," said Cochran, as they drove along. "Your new friend is bleeding to death in the neighbor's yard right now, I emptied my clip in him. You shouldn't have run away, sweetheart. When you run, people die. How selfish you are! Be nice now and let them live."

The chase through the yard had hurt her feet, not yet healed, but she had left her mark on one of the men, the one now in the passenger seat. He had gotten too close and she had delivered a kick she had learned in martial arts class. She would have gotten away, but for the other man, who was stronger than she realized and had played football, from the flying tackle he gave her.

"You can't do this! Do you have any idea what you have done already?" she whispered, sounding meeker than she thought she could.

Cochran laughed. Laughter came from the driver as well. The man in the passenger seat didn't laugh. He was still in pain from the kick to the jaw.

"You won't be any more trouble to us soon. Before long, you'll be as helpless as a baby, compliant and well-behaved. You're not dealing with Rossini and his cousins now. You're going to fulfill your destiny, to be the perfect little painted Japanese whore. You belong to me now and you will do what I tell you to do, or you will die a slow and horrible death. There will be no escape this time."

Suki fell into a deep, dark hole, despairing of her fate. Her eyes filled with tears, but she fought them back, not wanting to give anything to these men, not even the satisfaction of her tears. The scenery looked familiar as they drove back into downtown, back to the club where the nightmare had started. Suki's heart sank even further. She was not just in the grips of these men, she going back to the tattoo artist.

Inside the club stood the horishi, ready to continue his tebori, his hand-drawn tattoo. The horishi looked tired. He had a bruise on the side of his face and his eye was swollen.

He looked at Suki with hatred in his eyes, seeing her as the source of his recent trouble, seeing her also as his only way out of this job. He must finish and quickly if they are going to let him go. He only hoped, whether they paid him or not, he could go on his feet and not in a body bag. He didn't trust these people.

The horishi undressed Suki.

"I have to redraw the rest of the image," he said. "The lower part has been washed away."

"Just get to work," scowled Cochran. He turned to the other two and gave them an ultimatum, "If she gets out again, shoot her – or I shoot you."

Cochran went out into the dimly lit bar, over to the bartender station and poured a scotch and water. He drank it and looked back at the door.

This girl was too much trouble. She had cost him several men and had turned the attention of the police his way. She had brought in another player, a stranger, who had overpowered and shot his men – stupid men, but men he counted on, deserved or not.

He returned to the door, opened it and said to the Cadillac's driver, "Get a couple of more men over here, right away."

The man nodded and put a cell phone to his ear. Cochran closed the door. He sat at one of the tables, put the glass down hard and drummed his fingers.

"This is out of hand. I'm getting the idea I've made a bad deal. I don't like bad deals. They make me cranky."

Within twenty minutes, two sullen men in rumpled suits appeared at the door. The Cadillac driver spoke with them, then directed them over to Cochran. The two men came up to his table without a greeting, looking attentive. They were there to listen, not talk. Cochran did the talking.

"Go to Rossini's. Put this car back in his garage and clean up the other guy. If he's still alive, bring him back here. If he's dead, put him in Rossini's place. Then go to the kid's house, check on Walker and the other guy, see if the kid's back yet."

The two men nodded and left without comment. Cochran watched them leave, then turned to his driver, yelling:

"Get me some food in here. I'm starved."

C. J. Abbot

Carrie's Place

Shawn got up off the grass, amazed not to be covered in holes. His shirt was, but not him. A thousand thoughts raced through his head. The police would be there soon, there were shots fired in a populated neighborhood. The men had taken Suki and he didn't know where. He was alive for now, but they were not likely to be so kind again. The darkness crept over the city. It was late, he was hungry and his shirt was full of bullet holes.

Shawn ran to the GTO, jumped in and pulled the door shut. The aging classic groaned as he yanked it in gear. He realized, as he pulled out of the neighborhood, it had been 24 hours since he had first met Suki, back when she ran into his car in the rain.

The rain kept up. He still didn't know where the tattooed girl was. It was Saturday night and he had nowhere to go.

Hunger and rain were things to notice, but not to dwell upon. The only thing pressing on his mind. was where they had taken Suki. He needed to think!

He couldn't go back to Rossini's house, the police would be all over it. Getting stopped by the police now would be tragic.

Then an idea came into his head. Shawn spun the GTO around and headed out to Glendale. Just off Central he found the old-Hollywood style garden apartments he had seen only once, when he had been in a car with several people from work, including Carrie. "There's where I live," she had said. All eyes turned and looked at the attraction pointed out by tour guide Carrie. What once seemed like the least important piece

70

of information in Southern California now was Shawn's only anchorage. He pulled the car around back, to the one open spot.

"Visitor" was written in white paint, faded years ago and never repainted. He shut the engine and got out, listening. Down the central walkway, he listened for the sound of anything familiar. As he walked, he looked at the few, cheap items decorating one door, then another.

On the plate stuck in the ground in front of number fourteen, he saw a name painted: "Caroline." He stopped and knocked on the door. The door opened and Carrie looked out with surprise.

"Shawn?" she said, swinging the door wide.

"Hi, Carrie," said Shawn, walking in, not knowing what he would say next.

Carrie looked at Shawn as if she had never seen him before. Indeed, she had never seen him like this before. He had been in the rain, dressed in a shirt way too big for him and full of holes.

"Uh, are those bullet holes in your shirt?"

"It's not my shirt."

"O – K – But are you alright?"

"I don't know. I'll check."

Shawn felt his belly and chest, the part of his back he could reach, but didn't feel any pain, no blood, no holes deeper than the shirt he had stolen from Carlo Rossini's house.

"Nope, I think I'm OK."

"Well, what the...?"

"Can I sit down for a while?" Shawn slumped into a chair at the kitchen table.

"Yeah, I'll get you a glass of – something."

Carrie took an open bottle of red wine from the fridge, poured a glass and put it on the kitchen table in front of

Shawn. He looked at it and then took a drink. He still didn't know what to say. She looked at him, he could feel it; he had to say something.

"Missed you at work. Well, I miss you. I don't know if anyone else..." It seemed like a strange thing to say, but it was a strange day and he was in a strange mood.

"Shawn?" said Carrie.

"I didn't have a number for you and I did a search, but you're not listed anywhere. It would have been nice to talk to you. You left so suddenly."

"Shawn?" said Carrie again.

"Yeah?" Shawn stopped jabbering. He looked at Carrie, trying to make sense of the day, trying to think of a way to explain himself in a few words. It wasn't working.

"Shawn, why are you here?"

She pulled the shirt up to see several minor burns on his side, burns in long lines, made as the bullets passed close to his body. She let the shirt go and looked at him, her head tilted like a curious puppy.

"It's like this..."

Slowly, the story came out, the tale of a naked girl who ran into his car in the rain, the same car he had left on a street in the warehouse district with three wounded men, similar to the men who later took the girl. He had a stolen car, guns lay on the floor, he wore a stolen shirt and the tattooed girl was gone.

"So, is she a girlfriend?" asked Carrie.

"No, not a girlfriend," said Shawn, looking blankly into the space in front of him.

"Friends with benefits?" she asked.

"No, not that either. I don't know her, but I care for her, I feel responsible for her and I want to find her. She's in danger."

"OK, let's see to you first, after all, you're right here. Let's start with a shirt."

Carrie pulled the oversized shirt over his head and walked to the door in the kitchen. She dropped the shirt near the door and changed direction, heading to the bedroom. When she returned, she had a red and black plaid shirt of light cotton.

"Try this on. Old boyfriend. Don't ask!" Carrie rolled her eyes and made a face designed to explain it all. It explained nothing.

"Thanks," said Shawn, taking the shirt.

He looked at Carrie. He felt a sudden closeness with her he couldn't explain, more than just friends from the office or even friends with benefits, though they had never gotten to the benefits.

Carrie looked back, struck with a sudden need to be busy. She turned toward the kitchen, picked up the kettle and held it under the tap.

"What are you doing?" Shawn asked.

"Making tea. You want honey in your tea?"

"Sure. Honey." He continued to watch the girl who had taken him in and dressed him without hesitation or question.

Carrie was "Caroline," though no one was named Caroline these days. She was smart, but like him, not good in school, jumping from one to the next until she got a reputation as a wild card. After graduation she did the same thing with jobs. Carrie drove a Chevy. It said "Malibu" on the back, but he doubted anyone in Malibu drove one. She got fired overnight with no warning. It was the way things happened at his company. At first he was upset because he wouldn't see her anymore, then realized she wasn't an employee anymore, so rule number one didn't apply. When it occurred to him he didn't have her number, he returned to being upset. Now here he was, with her, but the circumstances didn't make for good conversation.

"So, now what?" Carrie asked, standing with her back to the stove as the water boiled. This was a new side of Shawn, one she had never seen. He was involved, up to his ears. This was important to him. It was kind of sexy.

"I don't know. I drove through the rain, hungry, no safe place to go, nowhere I could think. Tell the truth, I'm out of options, at the end of my rope. I lost her; I have to get her back. It's literally the first matter-of-life-or-death thing in my life."

He looked out of the door, still open, to the neighbor's kids playing in the deepening dusk. The neighbor's two little girls had a third over to play. They danced and laughed on the walkway in the rain as if there were no trouble in the world.

Then the fog cleared. Shawn sat up, a new light in his eyes.

"What?" asked Carrie, suddenly concerned.

"Les Girls, Girls, Girls! That's it!"

Shawn jumped to his feet, put his hands on Carrie's arms and kissed her hard. He spun out the door with words he should have delivered softly and under different circumstances.

"I love you!" and he was gone.

Carrie stood by the stove looking at the open door. She turned to the whistling tea pot and turned the flame off. From the back of the complex the roar of an engine and the squeal of tires told of Shawn's departure.

"To hell with the tea," she said, as she took a glass and filled it to the brim with red wine.

Les Girls, Girls, Girls

Two cocked pistols lay on the floor of the GTO. At a light, Shawn opened the glove box to find a third, the one Suki had put there, the one from Carlo Rossini, the one she shot him with. He took it out and put it on the floor with the other two.

Down Riverside Drive, he tried to remember the night club from the brief glimpses he had of it. Every light was too slow and too long, every Saturday night reveler was in the way. The rain didn't make it better.

Alameda was slick and dangerous, full of ancient pickups and slow-moving limos out on a Saturday night. No one seemed to want to go fast or get out of the way.

After what seemed to be an endless journey, he pulled up behind the club, Les Girls, Girls, Girls. The back door was locked and chained; the only way in or out was the front door.

The club was closed. It had been closed for months. In the battle between night club and local community center, the community center won – for now. There would be other days in court, but for the moment, nobody stripped in this neighborhood.

Shawn walked into the club with a gun in each hand and the third in his belt. He didn't slow his walk when he saw the two men sitting at a table drinking Jack Daniels. As they stood, reaching for their weapons, Shawn lifted his hands and began to fire. He fired two shots from the left-hand gun and two from the right. The one in his left hand clicked and stuck open; it was empty. Shawn reached for the gun in his belt as he fired with his right hand. It clicked open with the ejection of the

75

C. J. Abbot

shell and Shawn let it drop from his hand. He fired again with his left hand, shifted the gun in his right hand and continued firing.

As he stepped over the bodies of the two men, not even noticing if they were alive or dead, he picked up their guns and continued toward the back door. Shots came through the door and Shawn returned the fire through the closed door. He kicked the door open to see a third man lying on the floor. He looked up to see Suki lying on the tattooing table, the artist standing behind the table, quaking, the blood drained from his face. His hands were empty, having dropped his tools on the floor at the first shot. He was terrified!

Shawn looked at the man on the floor as he stepped over him. He wasn't dead, but wasn't going anywhere. The man on the floor moved to get up and Shawn shot him in the leg. A bullet in the leg had proven to be a distraction in the past and he was pleased to use it again. The man flopped back down, contorted in pain.

Shawn ran to the horishi, put the gun under his chin and pushed him to the wall behind.

"If you ever touch her again, it will be the last thing you do!" said Shawn in a low, cold voice.

The horishi froze. A large, dark stain appeared on his pants. His eyes rolled back in his head. Shawn let him go and the man sank to the floor.

Shawn turned to the table and saw Suki tied, the shirt was in tatters on the floor. On a side chair hung a robe, peach-colored and embroidered. Shawn picked it up and threw it over her shoulders. He pulled at the knots and they gave way.

Shawn drew Suki to him. She was weak, whimpering. She had been beaten. Her face and shoulders were bruised. Her bandaged feet showed fresh blood. Shawn picked her up and cradled her in his arms.

76

"Come on. Let's get out of here," said Shawn. He stepped over the moaning man at the door, shooting him in the other leg on the way. The man screamed and rolled in pain. The gun clicked open and Shawn dropped it.

Shawn carried Suki out to the GTO, put the her in the passenger seat and clicked her seat belt closed. As he settled in behind the wheel, he listened. Nothing – but not for long. He knew the police would be there soon. Shots fired. No doubt were getting used to it. Shawn started the car and put it in gear.

C. J. Abbot

Shots Fired at Les Girls

Sergeant Wentworth pulled up to the front door of *Les Girls, Girls, Girls* and sighed hard. He knew he was late. It had been minutes since the report of shots fired. He wondered what he would find this time.

Three cars responded to the report. One went around back as two others blocked the front of the club. Wentworth entered to find an officer holding three pistols.

"There are two more over there, Sarge, they appear to be the guns from the other guys, the one's before, the last place we were."

"Oh, good," said Wentworth. "So, we'll arrest whoever's prints are on those guns."

The officer looked at the guns, then at Wentworth. His face deflated and he looked at his shoes.

"Sorry, Sarge."

"Call the hospital, again. Tell them we need a bus, again. Tell them three patients, again."

"Shit!" said the officer, as Wentworth stepped past him, moving on to the next disaster. Wentworth shook his head and turned his attention to the two men on the floor.

"So who do we have here?" asked Wentworth to an officer kneeling over one of the wounded men.

"More of the same, no IDs. The guns appear to be all over the place. It'll take us a while to account for them all. All three of these guys have been shot but not killed. That's not usual."

"I'll take it over the alternative," said Wentworth.

"There's an Asian guy here. Want to see him?" called an officer from the back room.

"Oh, yeah," said Wentworth. "I want to see him."

Wentworth rolled his eyes. He couldn't believe how everyday ignorance turned to humiliating stupidity under stress. Crime scenes seemed to bring out the worst in his men. He wondered if he could fire them all and start again.

The horishi was brought forward, still shaking and soaked in his own pee.

"Jesus! Don't bring him so close. Take him over there and hit him with the water from the bar. Clean him up some. Ke-rist!"

The officers took the man behind the bar as Wentworth went into the other room to see the table. The ropes were there and pieces of cloth, torn, and tattoo artist tools laid out on a table.

"What's this for?" he yelled over his shoulder.

"Tebori," said the horishi, "ancient technique of tattoo by hand."

"Who?" asked Wentworth, grimacing at the thought.

"A girl. She is Japanese. They wanted her to look like it was done in Japan, not American."

"So they got you?" Wentworth took several steps across the barroom floor and cut the distance between them in half, making the horishi glad there was a bar still between them.

"There are other artists, but I was close and not busy. I was only to make the tattoo, nothing more."

"Couldn't you see she was unwilling?"

"Couldn't you see they had guns?"

Wentworth thought for a moment, then nodded. It made sense. If he didn't do what they wanted, they would kill him.

"Who is the girl?" Wentworth asked, softening.

"I don't know who she is. Her boyfriend owes money. She is payment. I don't know names."

"Where will I find these answers?"

"From them. They will tell you." The horishi nodded at the men on the floor, wounded but not dead.

Men in EMT uniforms rushed in with medical gear to care for the wounded men. Wentworth took one regaining consciousness and picked him up before the medics could get to him.

"Who is she? Who is the girl?"

"I don't know, Suni something," he moaned.

"You don't get care until you tell me."

"I don't know. I do what they tell me. Stand here, go there," he cried, half in anguish, half in pain.

"Kidnap her?"

The man paused, looked at Wentworth and then down.

"Yeah, if he says, or else I'm the one dead. You know how it goes, you refuse and it's the last thing you do."

Wentworth dropped the man. He screamed in pain. A medic came over with a dirty look for Wentworth.

"Yeah, yeah. Fix him up then you sympathizing sissy!"

Danny

Shawn drove up Alameda Boulevard, the only way he knew without thinking about it. He didn't need to think now, he needed to *think.* Suki lay sideways in the passenger seat, breathing but otherwise out of it.

The rain picked up and Shawn put on the wipers, slowing to let the speeders by him. "Angelinos are crazy," he thought, "driving in the rain as if they could." Everyone wanted to go fast. Moments before they crept along like snails.

"Danny," whispered Suki.

Shawn looked at her, then at the road, careful not to run into the crazy Angelinos. He looked for a place to pull over. Riverside Drive came up fast on his left, he took it, pulling onto the broad street next to the railroad tracks. Four cars were parked off to the side of the first block with a space in front. Shawn pulled up to the curb in front of the cars. He checked the mirror, in case there was a car behind, following. He figured if someone followed him, they would be trapped behind a bunch of parked cars.

He put the GTO in neutral and turned to the barely conscious girl.

"Suki?" he said, touching her head.

"My friend is Danny, lives in Eagle Rock, next to the freeway."

"Where, what street?"

"I have to see it to find it," she said, wincing.

"OK, Eagle Rock it is. We'll find it."

81

He pulled into the lane and up Riverside to Glendale Avenue, by Forest Lawn and up to Eagle Rock Boulevard. Suki pointed right, pulling herself up into a sitting position.

Shawn put on the headlights as the sky grew dark. The combination of rain and night cut visibility. People were being just as reckless, of course. Mindful of Suki next to him, Shawn drove slower, ignoring the cars around him.

At a street without a stoplight, Suki pointed left. Shawn turned and slowed to a crawl as Suki peeled her eyes for anything familiar.

"Here!" she said at a Craftsman house on the right. "In back," she pointed up the driveway.

Shawn pulled up the drive and parked behind a small, blue car. The symbol on the back proclaimed it as a Honda, considerably newer than his own poor Toyota, in the care of the Los Angeles police.

The rain had slackened to a steady drizzle as Shawn shut down the GTO and got out. He went around for Suki, who had opened the door, but otherwise had not moved.

"Come on," said Shawn, reaching to put both arms under her.

"No, wait, just give me a hand and I'll walk. Don't touch my back."

"OK." Shawn offered a strong hand and Suki pulled herself up, walking on bandaged feet, through the puddles to the small bungalow at the end of the driveway. The light from the windows looked warm and inviting.

Shawn knocked on the door and waited, Suki leaning on his arm. He heard a flush inside and a small figure approached the door. The curtain was pulled aside and a head appeared in the glass. Shawn could see the face register surprise. What looked to be a young Asian teenager opened the door.

"Danny," Suki whispered.

"Suki? Is that you?"

Shawn pushed through the door with Suki and put her on the couch. She sighed and slipped sideways onto the large pillow, a smile crossing her face. Danny looked at Shawn, then at Suki. Shawn could see he was trying to put it together.

"Long story," said Shawn. "Let's get her a blanket and some tea first, OK?"

"Yeah, OK," said a bewildered Danny, wandering into the bedroom.

Danny was small, the same size as Suki, in fact. He looked even smaller in an oversized tee shirt and a child's pajama bottoms. He was Japanese-American, many generations back, but like Suki, all the genes were small ones.

The bungalow bespoke of a high-tech, gizmo-oriented person bordering on genius, or maybe beyond the genius border. He wasted little money on furniture, as it clearly went into the gear displayed at the living room's focal point. Yet, for all the screens, players, recorders and amplifiers on display, none were on. Danny had been enjoying a tech-free weekend. Even the laptop on the kitchen table was closed. There was a soft scent of incense in the air.

Danny came out of the bedroom with a thin blanket. He covered Suki's bloody and tattooed back.

"Holy shit, Suki! Where'd you get that?" he asked. Danny looked concerned and curious, but when his gaze turned to Shawn, it was accusative.

"No, fella, not me. It was someone else. I spent all day trying to rescue her."

Danny accepted his brief explanation, turning his attention back to Suki.

"What do I do, Suki? What do you want? Should I call nine-one-one?"

C. J. Abbot

"No, Danny, thanks. I don't know. Maybe the police. We were on our way to the police. That's when we got caught – again, and escaped – again, and caught – again."

"It's been a long day. Got any soup?" asked Shawn.

"Yeah, I got soup," said Danny, surprised at the immediate solution being so easy and accessible. He got up and went to the kitchen.

"We've got to figure out what to do," said Shawn to Suki.

"I know. Let me rest and get something in my tummy, then we'll think."

Suki took Shawn's hand, closed her eyes, and winced from the pain in her arms and legs. Shawn kissed her on the head and sat on the floor, still holding her hand.

Soup and Decisions

Soup consumed and the tale told, Danny then filled a tub for Suki. She asked Shawn to put her into the tub and stay with her. He guessed she was friends with Danny, but not more. Shawn wasn't sure about his own relationship with the girl, but he knew he cared about her enough to steal a couple of cars and shoot a few people.

"Calling the police may not be our best idea," said Suki.

"Why not? I think it's a great idea, they'll have a doctor attend to you," said Shawn. He wasn't sure what they could do about the tattoo, but she had been beaten and confined. She needed attention.

"And they'll arrest you and we'll both be easy targets. How long could they have continued this sort of business without someone in or near the police? If you're in jail and I'm in the hospital, we'll be missing or dead before you know it. No, I'll stay here. And you'll stay here."

"They'll find the warehouse eventually, but for now it's safe. Though the thought going back through my neighborhood doesn't fill me with enthusiasm. Also, I don't have a key, so going back there could be futile."

"I know what you mean," said Suki, looking at her legs in the bath water.

"Is it bad?" She said as she leaned forward. She turned her head away from him, knowing there was no way the news could be good.

Shawn looked at her back. The flowering tree stretched across her shoulders and down her left side. The drawn lower

85

portion was gone, though the irritation to her skin from the drawing still showed red and angry. The fresh tattooing was covered with scabs. The latest addition, done just before Shawn burst into the night club, both guns blazing, was irritated and sore. For a moment, Shawn wished he had killed the tattoo artist. No matter what the incentive, positive or negative, he shouldn't have hurt this girl. Shawn tried to find a way to encourage her.

"You know, it's not bad. It's a beautiful tree. And once it settles out and heals some, I'm sure you'll want to show everyone."

"No, I won't. I'll want to do whatever it takes to get rid of it."

"Yes, of course. But I'll love you whatever you do."

He didn't know why he said it, but he knew he would let it stand; he wouldn't taking it back. And he wouldn't going to stammer and back-pedal, or say he was just kidding. He had known her a day and risked his life for her. He wouldn't leave her now. She was his first, last and only consideration. If it wasn't love, he didn't know what it could be.

Suki looked at him, feeling the warmth of his caring for her. Here was this man who didn't know her, yet was putting it all on the line. She had to tell him she saw it.

"I don't know what I feel. This is all too fast and too harsh for me, but I know no matter what else happens, I don't want to let go of you. Please don't leave me."

"I won't," said Shawn. He put a hand on her shoulder, careful not to touch any fresh part. He picked up the washcloth and squeezed water on her back, washing away the blood, dirt and perspiration, trying to wash away the day. They stayed there until the water was cold.

At last, she sighed and held out a hand. Shawn took it and helped her stand. He wrapped a bath sheet around her, lifted her into his arms and carried her to the living room. Danny pointed to the bedroom and guided Shawn in. He pulled the cover aside and brought more pillows. Soon, Suki sat in Danny's bed enjoying vegetable soup, spooned by Shawn.

"Should we go to the police?" asked Danny.

"We don't know what we're going to do, but we have to do something," said Shawn.

"I'm thinking, international kidnapping, racketeering and so on – the FBI will be your best bet. Why not go there? I bet they're open Sundays," offer Danny.

"Could be right. They might even overlook my stealing a couple of cars and shooting some guys."

Danny's eyes went up and his face went pale. "You shot someone?"

"Yeah, but they were bad people. They hurt Suki. It had to be done." Shawn didn't look up, raise his voice or stop spooning soup. It was a simple clarification.

Danny nodded, accepting this logic. "And stole a car," he added.

"Yeah, well, my car was kind of shot," he stopped to smile at this vernacular description, "so I took the guy's car and left him there for the police to find. And then we went to his place and swapped for his GTO."

"GTO?" Danny came alive, his eyes went wide, his eyebrows high in his forehead. "Where is it now, can I see it?"

"Yeah, it's out behind your Fit."

Danny jumped up and ran out into the darkness in his makeshift PJs. He walked around the GTO in the drizzling rain, then opened the driver door and got behind the wheel. He spent a good ten minutes touching everything before he came back inside.

"I love that car!" said Danny, dripping wet. He didn't care if he was wet; he actually sat in his dream car. He had been in love ever since he heard the Beach Boys sing "Little GTO."

"Listen, you can't drive it to see the FBI. How would it look? You've got to take my car and leave me the GTO for a while. You can tell the FBI it's safe. They'll collect it eventually, but what's the rush?"

"Danny, I don't know, these guys are not playing. If they see the car, they might shoot first and notice you're not me later."

"Well, we'll sleep on it" said Danny, "and see how it looks in the morning. For now, we need to rest and recuperate. Yeah, a little R&R is what you need."

Danny dried off and changed clothes, settling at the table with his laptop. When Suki was done with the soup, Shawn put the bowl aside and lay next to her, holding her in his arms until he felt her breathing even out. He laid her down on the pillow and stood over her for a moment before he walked out into the living room

"She's asleep," Shawn said to Danny.

"Kevin never was what you call a great choice, though his family is pretty well off. But to do this? He's off my Christmas card list, I'll tell you!"

Danny looked preoccupied with the computer. Shawn looked over his shoulder.

"I'm trying to find some noise on this," said Danny. "I can't find anything except some halfhearted attempts by Kevin to find Suki. He says she's run off after they had a 'little tiff' – Ha! A little tiff he calls it. When the word gets out he won't have a place to hide."

"Let's not put the word out just yet," said Shawn, afraid Danny might give away their location.

"No, not yet. It's time to stay low. I'll sleep on the couch. She feels comfortable with you."

Danny regarded Shawn with a look of trust. Shawn made a fist and touched it to Danny's shoulder, then he went back into the bedroom, laid down next to Suki and fell fast asleep.

C. J. Abbot

Five A.M.

It was still dark. Danny had been tossing in his sleep. The couch looked like a fight took place on it. In the past, he'd fallen asleep on the couch and had slept soundly, but tonight there was a GTO on his mind – and in his driveway.

At five in the morning, Danny couldn't take anymore. He was wide awake and all he thought about was the blue GTO convertible Shawn had driven to his house and just left, untended, behind his Fit. He had spent all night in his dreams, going through the gears on Mulholland Drive, the top down and the wind blowing through his hair. The dream had continued after he had woken up, unable to sleep. He had to see her, he had to feel her. He could no longer restrain himself. Danny got up and put on his clothes, grabbed a light jacket and went outside, taking the key to the GTO.

There sat the baby-blue beauty, glistening in the morning rain. She looked like she could get a speeding ticket standing still. Danny fell more and more in love by the minute.

He walked around the object of his desire, running a finger along the lines of the side and front fender. He looked inside through the rain-speckled window to the driver's seat. He could feel a tingling in his stomach and his head was light. He walked around the left front fender, keeping his eyes on the drivers' seat, then opened the door and sat – just for a moment – feeling his slender frame cradled in the black leather. He adjusted the seat all the way forward so his feet would reach the gas and brake, just to get the feel of her.

Then, Danny looked down at his hand. There was the key, dangling from the key ring he had slipped onto his pinky finger. He hadn't intended to drive her, only look her over. He had brought the key just in case. Now she invited him to warm her up, begged him to not hold back, to not deny her. He started the engine, just to hear her rev, to hear her moan and feel her hot breath.

A tremor went through him as he slipped her into gear and felt the transmission engage. He backed the car out of the driveway and into the street – not to drive her – but just to feel how she handles. There were sparklers in his head; he had to pay attention to every action, to tell himself to apply the brake with a soft touch, to not let her scrape on the steep angle of the driveway to the street.

Danny thought about the freeway behind him, it would be nearly empty on a Sunday at five in the morning. He thought about the GTO. Nobody would notice her, nobody would care if he had taken her, if he was inside of her and had his hands on her. He put the GTO in gear and crept down to the stop sign at the corner, a tingling in his fingers, a red flush on his face.

There was no one on Colorado Boulevard; all the lanes were empty. Danny looked both ways, revved the engine a couple of times and gunned it. He felt a thrill at the power surging under the hood. He pushed through the yellow light at the corner and headed for the freeway on-ramp. He fishtailed around the corner, regained control, went right on red at the on-ramp and up onto the empty freeway. He sailed past the broken boulder the town of Eagle Rock was named for and headed toward Pasadena, screaming at the top of his lungs.

As the clock on the dash clicked to seven exactly, Danny drove down another piece of empty concrete: Broad Street, downtown Los Angeles, the busiest shopping district in town. But it was Sunday morning; no one was out.

He had been tooling around L.A. For two hours and showed no signs of slacking, except he was low on gas. He pulled into a station, not paying any attention to the listed price – Danny didn't care what the gas cost, he would blow it out regardless. He pumped the gas wishing some friend would drive by and see him filling up a classic GTO convertible. He tried to think who it would be. Perhaps someone from work, though what they would be up at this hour or in this neighborhood, he couldn't guess.

A police car passed, slowing as it did. Danny turned away and stopped pumping. They might be looking for her. He hadn't thought of that. What had Shawn and Suki said? They took her from the home of someone Shawn had shot.

Oops! Is this a stolen car? And oops! Was there a gun on the floor? He leaned to his left, trying to look into the car to see if there was a gun visible. He couldn't tell. He hoped he wasn't going to get searched. The police car continued to drive down the street, apparently looking for something else not quite fitting in.

Danny took the receipt, in case they might trace him through it, and opened up the driver's door. The gun was not there on the floor, nor under the seat; not in the glove box and not in the back. Then Shawn must have taken it inside with him. Danny shuddered to think about Shawn sitting there talking to him with a loaded gun in his pocket. Did Suki know?

The police car disappeared into the distance. Danny let out a breath and slipped into the driver's seat once more. Now where? Olvera Street popped into his head. They would be just starting the coffee and tacos at the stands up and down Olvera Street.

The first street in the pueblo of Los Angeles now lay between Main Street and Los Angeles Street. If he got there before the early morning rush, he might find a close parking spot where he could watch the car while having his coffee and a breakfast taco. Danny gunned the little GTO as the light turned green and headed for Olvera Street. She seemed to purr in agreement with the decision.

By the cobbled square, just as the vendors set up, there was plenty of space at the curb across from the fountain. Danny got out of the GTO and looked up at the drizzling rain. He sauntered across the street to the square and the fountain. At the fountain, he turned and looked at her, waiting patiently at the curb for him to return, promising to stay warm for him.

He turned toward Olvera Street with coffee on his mind, past the old office building at one side of the square. In the overhang, sitting on the steps to the second floor, was a small group of Latinos. One of them was a girl, Danny noticed, about the same size as Suki, about the same size as him. He looked at the girl, she looked at him as well. One of the members walked over to him. But he was not small like him, he was big.

"Hey, your car?" he said, indicating the GTO.

"Yeah, it's my car," said Danny, raising his head, slowing his step. It was a reaction left over from school: don't show them you're afraid and they might just leave you alone.

"Man, one sick rag-top! How'd you score a gem like that?"

"Belongs to a friend of mine," said Danny, thinking they might not steal it if he could conjure a scary enough friend.

Danny could see tattoos at his neck and arms. Large tattoos peeked out of his shirt at the neck line. He continued walking toward the little coffee and taco stand just a few spaces in, one of the double row of small stands selling Mexican items to attract the tourists.

"You mind if we take a look?" asked the large, tattooed man. Danny faltered, stopped, trying to not break a sweat. What harm could they do, after all? They admired the car, and him for having it. They surely wouldn't scratch it or damage it in any way.

"Sure, check her out. She's open," said Danny, returning to his bee-line toward coffee and away from the large and colorful people admiring his ride. He wondered why he had been so quick to give permission, but he had and he couldn't take it back.

Turning out of the warehouse district, a large black Cadillac sedan drove toward the restaurant district just the other side of Olvera Square.

"Isn't that Rossini's GTO? Didn't he have a blue GTO convertible?" asked the man in the shotgun seat.

"Yeah, the guy took when we shot him," said the driver, slowing down.

"Pull over here. Who's inside it?" asked the man behind the driver.

Across the street, in the driver's seat of the GTO, sat a large, tattooed man. On the sidewalk were four other men and three girls, all with similar tattoos and kerchiefs.

The Cadillac pulled up to the curb and stopped. Three men got out holding pistols. One of the gang members looked up and saw them.

"Suits," he said. All heads turned toward the three armed men.

"Where'd you get the car?" ask the driver.

"Chinga-te, Pendejo!" yelled the leader of the group.

The three men in suits raised their guns and fired. The man behind the wheel fell to the side and crawled out of the open side door onto the sidewalk. The others ducked behind the car, crouching as bullets shattered the windows and riddled the door and fenders.

The three gunmen emptied their pistols, sending two dozen rounds into the GTO.

When they were done, the men stood with their guns locked in the open position, empty, as the dust settled in the street. The Latinos walked out from behind the GTO. It was their turn. They raised their arms and the three gunmen found themselves facing eight loaded pistols.

"You pendejos don't know how to shoot," yelled the leader. Then he pointed his pistol and cried, "Uno!"

Eight pistols fired as one, with a single "Crack!" to count for all of them. The three men dropped to the ground, their empty pistols clattering on the pavement.

"Now, that's what I'm talking about!" said the leader. There were nods of agreement and approval all around when the leader looked at the black sedan.

"Say, man, what is that, a Cadillac?" he asked.

"Yeah, it's a Cadillac," said another man.

"Well, I like Cadillacs." The leader began walking toward the car, followed by the rest. They got into the sedan and drove off, leaving the three gunmen in the street and the little blue GTO full of holes.

In the distance, a siren whined, growing louder and louder. Behind a covered kiosk, Danny poked his head out to see the GTO sitting on flat tires, the door, fenders and top full of holes and the windows shot out. On the street were three men in suits with empty guns on the concrete beside them.

Danny pulled his head back and slumped on the ground. The smell of fresh coffee and cooking tacos filled the air, but Danny didn't notice; he couldn't breathe.

Olvera Square

Sergeant Wentworth got out of the squad car and stood with his hands on his hips looking at the scene. An officer checked the men in the street.

"You'll never believe this!" said the officer. "These men are alive. Shot up, but alive – for now."

"Call for a bus, let's get these guys collected. I want to find out what the hell's going on here." Twice in as many days he had found men lying in the street, shot but not dead, their car missing, another car close by, disabled and full of bullet holes. It had become a familiar scene and he was bored with it already.

The uniformed officer made the call for an EMT unit as another police cruiser pulled up. Wentworth walked toward the scene, looking with experienced eyes.

"What did they drive here and where is it now?" he asked himself out loud. "And who was in the Pontiac? Why is there no blood on it?" He looked around, expecting to see a small Japanese girl standing close by sporting a fresh tattoo. He didn't see any.

"Who keeps saving her?" He turned to look at the GTO, riddled with bullets. He counted bullets, trying to make sense of it all. "Yeah, about three clips. The guys in the street fired those. Who did this to them?"

He turned to the three bodies, two of them now moaning as they came to. In the distance, another siren stirred the air.

Wentworth knew the ambulances were on the way. Soon these men would be collected and seen to, charged and taken into custody. They would be questioned and would ask for lawyers. Their rights would be respected and they would be out on bail as soon as they were able to walk. The police would be left with nothing – again.

"I want everything from their pockets," Wentworth yelled at his officer, who looked up and nodded. The officer went through the pockets of the nearest wounded man as the first ambulance pulled up. Medical teams jumped to patch up the gunmen so they could be alive to get their lawyers and bail. Wentworth knew it wouldn't be soon, given their wounds. He cracked a crooked smile at the thought.

The officers from the second squad car went to question the people in the square. Onlookers gathered at the mouth of Olvera Street, neglecting their setup duties to catch a glimpse of the lead story they would see later on the morning news.

A second ambulance arrived and two more squad cars. Uniformed officers and EMTs swarmed over the square. Yellow tape fluttered between parking meters. More people came to watch, others left rather than be questioned by police. In the middle of it all, Danny stood in shock, not knowing which way to go next.

"Did you see who did the shooting, sir?" asked a uniformed officer. Danny just looked at the scene before him, wondering how he would tell Shawn the GTO was shot up and the police were all over it.

"Sir? Did you see who shot these men?" repeated the officer.

"Hm? Uh, no, I didn't. I went for coffee, it was already done when I got here. Are those men...?" Danny pointed at the men in the street.

"No, sir," said the policeman. "They're wounded is all. They'll live."

"Oh. OK." Danny turned around and wandered down Olvera Street still in a daze. The officer shrugged and went to question another person.

A couple of miles to the South, Cochran sat in a Town Car on Alameda Boulevard. He looked at the police tape strung across his night club and wondered where his men in the Cadillac were. He looked at his watch, it was eight in the morning, too early for everything to go wrong.

"They should have reported in by now," he said to the driver, Mason. Mason didn't respond. He just looked in the mirror at his boss in the back seat.

In Eagle rock, Shawn turned over, surprised to find Suki looking at him, wide awake. He smiled at her. She smiled back.

"I didn't want to get up, didn't want to wake up Danny," she whispered.

"OK if we just lie here for a while, you know, together?"

"Yeah, OK."

The Boyle Heights Lobos

Danny sat at a table at the east end of Olvera street, looking at a cup of coffee. He was completely at a loss for what to do. He had fallen in love and had lost her within a few hours. His heart was broken by a baby-blue GTO convertible and he was inconsolable. He would have to go back and tell Shawn what had happened. He didn't even know how he would get back; he was stuck at Olvera Street without a ride.

Traffic picked up as churches began morning services. The stream of life on the street of vendors wasn't disrupted by the sirens breaking the morning silence. Most people who heard the sirens weren't around to hear the gunshots just before. For most folks, the day was just starting. For Danny, the day was four hours old and he just got coffee. He knew if he had arrived at the square just a few minutes later, he would be the one full of holes instead of the classic Pontiac. The poor little GTO sat at the curb, surrounded by police putting every piece of trash and unidentified smudge into plastic envelopes, sealing them with red tape. The plastic envelopes were put into bags, labeled and placed into a box.

Danny sat at a small table at the other end of Olvera Street trembling from the incidents of a few minutes earlier. He didn't notice the black sedan pulling up to the curb near to him until it was already parked. Two large, Latino men got out of the car, picked Danny up and carried him to the car. The Cadillac pulled away from the curb and executed a perfect illegal u-turn across Alameda Boulevard. Danny sat in the back seat between two laughing gang members. In the front seat, the one he had first met drove. Two girls sat next to the driver. One was as tall as Danny.

The Cadi drove to a local bodega and parked by the curb in front. The driver turned off the engine and the six of them sat there in silence.

"Man, this car is sick!" exclaimed the wheel man. He turned to the two girls. "Ladies, would you give us a minute with our friend?"

Without a word, the two girls got out. A man who seemed to be the leader got in, turning in the seat to look at Danny.

"I'm Julio," said the man in the front seat. He was dark with a thin mustache and a scar over his eye. There was a tear tattooed by the scar. He wore a red bandana on his head.

"Pirate-style," thought Danny.

Julio just looked at him, waiting. Danny snapped to, realizing he had been addressed and was expected to respond.

"Uh, I'm Danny. Pleased to meet you."

"OK, Danny. A black sedan filled with men in suits and holding guns shot at us for no reason. Twice in a couple of days. The only clue we have is you. So tell me, my new friend, what's the story?"

Danny smiled. Julio seemed friendly enough, but firm. The other guys didn't pull any weapons or threaten him, they just sat there being dangerous.

"My – my friend showed up late last night with the car and I wanted to take it for a ride – I mean, it's a GTO! How could I not take it for a ride?"

"I completely understand. So! Your friend. Exactly who is your friend?"

"A friend. A friend of mine. We have a lot in common. We go way back. She's Japanese too, like me."

"Little?" asked Julio. He looked at the man in the driver's seat, who looked back, like something just fell into place.

"Yeah, she's short, like me." Danny wasn't getting the connection.

"She on the run from somebody?" asked Julio.

"Yeah," said Danny, darkening. "Her sleazebag boyfriend traded her to some bad guys. She got away."

"Alone?" asked Julio.

"She's got a guy helping her. He looks OK."

Julio and the other man exchanged looks again and nodded approval.

"Where's this girl now?"

"I left them at my place, sleeping. I only took the car for a joy ride. I never meant for it to be destroyed. He's gonna be pissed."

"We'll 'splain it to him. C'mon, we're gonna give you a ride home."

Julio made a small gesture and the driver started the engine and looked in the rear view mirror at Danny.

"Where to?" he asked.

Danny gulped hard. "Eagle Rock."

"We're the Boyle Heights Lobos. Nobody messes with us," said Julio as they drove. "Some pendejos in suits come into our house and start shooting, they gonna get some lead back – just like those hijo-des back there."

Danny sat in the back, gripping his knees. The Cadi's clock said nine-forty-five. He had opened his big mouth and was now on the way to his place with armed gang members in a stolen car. The last stolen car was sitting at Olvera Square surrounded by policemen.

"The guys Friday night thought our little Lacra was somebody else and wanted to take her." Julio looked at Danny for a response.

"They might have thought she was my friend, Suki."

"Yeah." Julio looked at the driver, as if the conclusion had already been jumped to, then turned his attention to the road ahead. The rain continued in a thin drizzle.

"How about this rain. Just enough to be a pain in the ass," said Julio to no one in particular. Both of the other gang members nodded their heads.

"This is Hector," said Julio, indicating the man in the driver's seat. "That's Jesus and Alfredo." The man next to Danny looked at him without smiling. Danny nodded to him, hoping it would be enough.

Hector reached to the radio and pushed the knob. The Spanish station came up immediately, loud and garish. They had already found it and had reprogrammed the buttons. Twin horns in harmony blared out a passage and all three nodded to the rhythm. When the words came in, all three sang along. Danny was caught between two worlds, riding in a gangster car with three Boyle Heights Lobos.

"Why do you want to find my friend?" he ventured.

"Because we want to help her," said Julio, without looking back.

"Why would you do that?" asked Danny.

Julio turned around, looking serious. "Because the enemy of my enemy is my friend. That's why." Hector, Jesus and Alfredo all nodded. They were in this together.

Wake up call

"He's not here!" said Suki with her eyes wide. She was wrapped in a sheet, picking up clothing.

"Is his car here?" asked Shawn.

"His is, the GTO is gone," said Suki, looking with worried eyes at the strips of bloody clothing she held in her hands.

"Now, let's get a grip. If anyone had come and taken him, we'd know. My guess is he took the GTO for a joy ride. He should be back any minute. Let's calm down and have breakfast."

He looked at the girl-child, standing draped in a sheet, in near tears, and his heart broke into little pieces. She had her whole world ripped away overnight and it got worse as the days roll on.

"Look," he said, comforting her. "I'll make us something to eat, you find something of Danny's you can wear – he looks about your size – and he'll be back in no time. If he's taken the car to Vegas, he'll call. We'll take his car and go to the FBI. It'll work out; you'll see."

Shawn hoped he sounded convincing. He had convinced himself at least. It was an awful lot to heal in a couple of sentences. Breakfast would help.

As he tinkered in the kitchen, figuring out Danny's coffee maker, searching for where he kept the various makings, Suki rummaged through Danny's clothes for something to fit and still not make her look like Danny. She found jeans and a tee shirt, a throw-over shirt of blue checks and a pair of canvas deck shoes. These she laid out on the bed as she considered a shower.

As Shawn started toast and eggs, he heard the familiar sound of the shower and smiled. A few minutes later, the water was turned off and he could hear Suki in the bedroom. When she came to the door, she looked like a tomboy.

"Breakfast is served," he said with a flourish.

Suki smiled. "Thank you, sir. I could get used to this service. You'll spoil me."

Shawn could still hear a tremor in her voice. The fear was hidden, but not gone. He smiled and performed a small bow.

"A pleasure, m'lady. It is an honor to serve."

Suki sat quiet for a moment, savoring the eggs and toast, coffee and orange juice, looking like a child lost among the big-people's tableware.

"Do you think they'll be watching my place?" she asked, big eyes looking up at him.

"I would if it were me," said Shawn. Suki darkened.

"It would be nice to have some of my own clothes and some makeup," she sighed.

"You look fine. If you want, we'll stop and get you some makeup, but you look great. You don't need makeup."

She did look great. Her hair was pulled back instead of styled, but she was pretty without makeup, fresh and clean.

The clothes fit her, though they were made for a boy. Danny shopped in the boy's section. With a hat, her hair tucked in, she could pass for a boy. He was about to suggest a disguise when Suki looked up at him.

"What if the police picked him up?" she said, her eyes wide.

"Then they would be here, questioning us. He didn't steal the car. And he wouldn't take the rap for us. He knows we're not the bad guys here. The police don't have him."

"Then those other guys do," said Suki, turning her head away, not wanting to think about the possibilities.

"No, not at all. He's joy riding. He's at some drive-in restaurant talking up some waitress about how he's a collector and just felt like it was a GTO day. Trust me, he'll come back with a smile on his face and lipstick on his collar."

Shawn hoped it was true. Suki went back to her breakfast while he looked around the room. There was Danny's laptop. He could get online and do a search. Shawn got the computer and set it up next to his breakfast plate. He came up with an address for the California Bureau of Investigation.

"There's an office in L.A., on Wilshire Boulevard. I know where it is. If Danny's not back soon, we'll take his car. It'll be fine."

Suki curled up on the couch and looked out at the rain, reflecting on current events. She was in Danny's clothes, house and car, with a man she had just met, with a painful tattoo across her back and gangsters looking for her. She wished she could just go back to Friday and break up with Kevin before he could sell her to the sex-slave trade.

Now it was anger she felt. How dare he? Coward! Bastard! She wanted to drive up to Kevin in a black sedan and get out with a pistol, to empty the clip and watch him go down with pleading eyes.

"A little tiff, my ass!" she muttered under her breath.

"What?" said Shawn, not sure what he heard.

"Are we going to do this, or what?" asked Suki, getting up with an attitude. She picked a jacket from the coat rack by the door and put it on. Shawn figured breakfast was over and the dishes would remain on the table for now.

Back on the Road

Shawn found the keys to the Honda Fit hanging on a hook next to the door. He picked up the remaining pistol, just in case.

Suki looked out. Sure enough, there was the Fit, but no GTO. Of course, there were no black sedans with men in suits with guns. Which was good news. She had far too much to do with those stereotypes of late.

Suki stepped out into the drizzle, followed by Shawn, who stepped around her to open the car door. He held it for her and closed it once she was in, then went around. It wasn't to impress her he was a gentleman, but he didn't want her doing anything on her own, without him there to protect her, including getting into a car.

Shawn pulled onto Colorado Boulevard just as the black Cadillac turned off onto the side street. Shawn saw Danny's face in the back, between two large bodies.

"It's Danny and he didn't look good," said Shawn, flooring the Honda, taking the curve too wide, nearly clipping another car. The angered driver honked and gave Shawn the finger. Shawn smiled when he saw the gesture. In the past few days, except for Suki, the finger was one of the nicest things he had been given.

The Cadillac spun around and came after them, right through the stop sign without slowing. They caught up to Danny's Fit and motioned for him to pull over. Shawn stepped on the gas.

"He doesn't want to be caught," said Julio in the Cadillac.

"He thinks we're the other guys," said Danny.

Again neck and neck, Danny leaned over Jesus and hung out of the window.

"It's OK, pull over," he yelled at Shawn.

Shawn made a decision to trust Danny and drove the Fit to the curb. Hector pulled in front of him and stopped. Shawn put the pistol in his belt, ready to bring it out if this turned out to be something else. Danny came running.

"It's OK, these guys are friends. Follow us." Danny ran back to the sedan. Shawn could see the man in the front seat put a phone to his ear just before the sedan pulled into traffic, continuing up Colorado Boulevard. At a wide place, the sedan made a u-turn and headed in the other direction. Shawn followed, hoping there wasn't a police car hiding within view of the traffic violations. The jig could be up over an illegal turn.

Hector pulled into Linda's Cafe on Colorado Boulevard and around to the back. Shawn followed, parking next to the big Cadillac.

Danny and the Boyle Heights Lobos got out of the Cadillac, went to the back door to the cafe and turned to look at Shawn still sitting in the Honda Fit. Danny came over to the car. He opened the passenger side door and offered a hand to Suki.

"My clothes fit you? How embarrassing, but I'm glad. You look good. Come in. These guys are cool."

Suki took Danny's hand. Shawn got out, slipping the pistol into his back pocket and pulling his shirt-tail over it. He walked behind Danny and Suki, so as to not let them see the pistol making a bulge under his shirt.

"Linda," called out Jesus, "We're gonna use the back room, can we get some coffee?"

A dark haired woman in waitress pink waved and picked up a tray. Jesus knew where the light switch was and the back room, usually reserved for special occasions, was in service.

Another car stopped outside and Hector got up to see.

"Berto," he said, sitting back down.

"I hope you don't mind, we called a few friends to come and help us sort this out," said Julio, commanding the end of the table. A man and three women came in, taking chairs. The third woman was barely a girl, small, in a jacket far too big for her. She sat across from Suki, making eye contact. Suki couldn't see a smile, but she didn't feel a threat either.

"This is Lacra," said Julio. All eyes turned to the short girl. She looked each right in the eye, defiant. Shawn knew she also had a pistol. Julio let her name and presence sink in, then continued.

"Lacra is my sister. Nobody messes with Lacra, or they mess with me."

"And nobody messes with Julio," added Lacra.

Shawn nodded. "I see. When men shot at you Friday night in the rain. They thought Lacra was Suki." He gestured toward Suki.

Lacra and Suki exchanged glances. Two petite girls with black hair and delicate features who, at a glance, could be sisters. Suki's raven hair fell forward, covering her bruised and battered face, just as Lacra's sable locks fell across her face. One would have to pull those curtains back to see they were different people.

"I think so," said Julio. "So why do they want her?"

Suki turned red and dipped her head. Kevin's deal was the humiliation of her life.

"It's a bad scene," said Shawn. "Her fiancé owed money. He traded her for the debt. She was to be passed off as a prostitute from Japan." Shawn looked at Suki, "Show them!"

Around the table, all heads turned to Suki, who stood, opening her coat and the shirt beneath. She turned, slipping the shirt down to reveal the tattoo across her back. She pulled the shirt back up and zipped the jacket up tight, sitting again, leaning into Shawn for comfort and support. Danny stood up behind her chair, his hands on her shoulders.

The response from the Boyle Heights Lobos was not what they expected.

"Aw-right, mama!" said Julio, unbuttoning the top button on his shirt, letting it fall behind him. He raised his tee shirt and underneath was a large tattoo, sprawling across his chest. Hector, Jesus, Fernando and Berto did the same. Pictures, words and religious symbols abounded across their bodies. They admired one another, approving and pointing.

"Come on, girls," said Julio – the only one, Shawn thought, who could say so, since Lacra was his sister.

Lacra and the other two girls stood and started to strip. Coats and shirts hit the floor as they stood there in the back room of the restaurant in their bras. Each was covered with tattoos, mostly the same, religious symbols and boyfriend's names.

Across her back Julio's sister had the word "Lacra" inscribed in a flourishing hand. When the girl turned around, she could see a large scar across her chest. As Lacra pulled her hair back, Shawn and Suki could see the scar continue up the side of her face and near to her left eye.

"Nice ink," said Shawn. "But you made the decision and got ink that means something to you. This was not her choice. This mark means she's property, to be pimped out for sex against her will."

"Some of it is a decision," said Julio. "Some, like Lacra's, is earned."

Lacra let her hair fall back over her face and pulled her shirt back on. The other two girls put on their shirts as well. Julio continued, a quiet anger under his soft words.

"We nearly lost her. It was a boy who came after me with a knife. Lacra got in the way. That was back when we called her 'Angelita.' Now she is called Lacra – it's her name."

"What does your name mean?" asked Lacra to Suki.

"It's short for my last name, but in Japanese slang Suki means 'like' – as in 'I like you,'" said Suki. It had been a long time since anyone asked. Lacra nodded.

"Lacra means 'Scar.'"

"Tell her your poem," said Julio.

Lacra stood up as all eyes turned toward her. She began in a strong voice, her fist high in the air.

Scar

Call me Scar:
I'm a cautionary tale,
The last remnant a broken family,
A pale reminder of a people
Torn from their homeland.
Call me Scar:
I am a marker for what was,
Rough at the edges and empty in the middle,
Scorched earth where something fine once stood.
Scar,
Hard and unbending,
Stiff and cold to the touch,
An ugly symbol saying, "Here is a story."
I am Scar,
Cover me with clean cloth,
Patch over me so you can forget
Wrap me up, so you can move on.
Scar,
Slather me in antiseptic,
Entomb me in a cast,
Conceal me away from polite society.
For I am Scar,
All that's left of an old wound,
The artifact of a nearly forgotten lesion,
An ancient trauma, historic hurt, an old harm.
Scar,

Rejected for being unsightly,
Hidden away as you would an ugly child,
A constant admonishment of a regrettable sin.
Of old wrongs, of unspeakable injustices,
Lessons learned, enlightened people,
And as a grim reminder
Point to me,
And call me Scar.

Lacra sat. The room was silent. Shawn felt a lump in his throat. He saw a tear roll down Suki's cheek. Danny fought back a tear, not wanting to look weak in front of the men.

One of the ladies put a hand on Lacra's shoulder. The other put her arms around the girl, but Lacra herself was still hard and resolved, looking straight at Suki. Suki looked back with compassion, wanting to hug the girl, but she knew it wasn't going to happen.

"So you see," said Julio, "We all bear the mark, the mark of our faith, the mark of our heritage, and the mark of our history."

Shawn looked at Julio, defiant.

"She was given a mark she didn't ask for, I can't let it go. I have something for the man who ordered this to be done," said Shawn, pulling the pistol from his back pocket and laying it on the table.

The gang members reacted, surprised he had a pistol, that he would draw it in public and in their presence. It surprised Suki and Danny as well. This was a side of Shawn they had not seen.

Julio looked at the pistol and nodded. He understood.

"Hector and Berto had my back when I went up against the man who gave my sister her name. Who has your back?"

Shawn looked from face to face around the table. He knew each one of them had a similar weapon, including the little girl who had so movingly delivered her poem. He knew these men and women were not his people, but now they had something in common.

"Perhaps you will," he said.

Surprised faces turned to Julio. Jesus raised his eyebrows, saying a sentence in a glance. Julio smiled.

"You got it, bro," said Julio.

The somber mood broke as Julio and Shawn stood up and shook hands, looking into each others eyes. They were bound now, as they never would have been if they had just met on the street.

Coleman

Coleman had been up all night, going through the events of the previous day. The girl slipped Rossini's grip, a car appeared and disappeared again while Rossini's men exchanged glares with a local gang. Coleman shook his head; to think this job could ever have been given to Rossini and his cousins. Now he stood in the middle of the warehouse district on a cold and wet Sunday morning. He pulled out a phone and punched a number. He put the phone to his ear, looking down the street in each direction.

"Mr. Cochran?" said Coleman into the phone. The low grunt meant Cochran her him. "I found the place they went. It's a warehouse, probably converted inside. I think they'll come back here."

"Get hold of Walker and his friend. No more mistakes. I'm getting tired of this. I'm coming too."

Coleman made a call to Walker and the new man, Surroyan, who sat on the boyfriend's place.

"Naw, he never showed," said Walker. "We've been here all night. We don't know where he's gone."

Coleman knew the boy wouldn't make it easy.

"Get over here, near the night club, look for my car. They'll show up here and we'll have 'em."

There were too many shot up men and cars. The city was getting hotter. Sooner or later, the police would put them together with the string of shoot-outs and the kidnapping of a Valley Debutante for the sex-slave trade. It would be too much to cover up.

Coleman walked around the warehouse. He looked in the broken window in the back. It was dirty in the warehouse, the dust hadn't been disturbed for a long time, save for a few footsteps, recent ones. Further up front, it was clean; someone regularly opened the door, disturbing the dust. It might even have been swept clean in front, but not in back.

Coleman stood back, looking up. The rain had stopped for now, but not for long. When L.A. decided to rain, it didn't stop; it rained until the concrete river became a raging torrent.

The building was one-story in back, but had a second story in the front half of the building. He climbed up onto the window of the adjacent building, up the ironworks to a fire escape and onto the roof. He walked to the windows in the rear of the second floor. at a place where the drapes parted, he looked in to see a workbench and a kitchen table. In the other corner, a bed. He smiled. This is where they had come. This is where, sooner or later, they would come back.

Coleman didn't think Cochran would kill the girl. He went over it in his head as he climbed back down to the alley. The guy who had saved her was a decision already made. He had seen too much and was too deep in. Leaving him alive was just plain out of the question. But the girl was still a payday to be realized.

On the other hand, the girl had escaped several times. Each time there was gunfire and lost resources, both men and vehicles. Cochran might consider he had been paid in coin of no value, too much trouble to cash in. He would simply eliminate the source of the trouble and go back to the boyfriend. He smiled as he imagined Cochran saying, "The girl didn't work out. You're still on the hook for the debt. What else you got to pay off with?" The boy would go pale and his knees would give way. He would either come up with another girl or would tap his family. After all, the boy came from money.

Of course, the girl's parents had money and might ransom her, but kidnapping for ransom was a whole other kettle of fish and involved factions of the FBI he didn't want to even think about. Besides, they could never let her go, no matter who paid what. The girl couldn't be allowed to tell her story, Cochran could never allow it. No, letting her go was not an issue for debate. She would be drugged into submission and put into service – or killed.

Coleman walked down to the side street where his car was parked. He drove a block away, where he could watch the place from across an empty lot, from a distance. He knew this neighborhood by now. The thought made him sneer. He only had one purpose: recapture the girl and the guy helping her. Once done, he never wanted to see these lousy streets again.

Friends with Benefits

The pact was made. New friends nodded, reaffirming they were strong together. Shawn, Danny and Suki were now honorary members of the Boyle Heights Lobos.

"Where to?" asked Danny, getting into the driver's seat of the Fit.

"My place," said Shawn. "We don't have a key, but I do have an idea. Once we're inside, it'll be like we never existed. There might even be police tape outside to keep out inquisitive people. We'll figure out a next step from there."

Shawn got into the rear seat where he could put an arm around Suki.

"So, you and Julio are friends now?" asked Danny.

"Yeah, we're friends – with benefits," answered Shawn, smiling wryly.

"What benefits do you mean?"

"The benefit that if anyone comes after me, Julio will shoot them."

"And..." Danny pulled onto the street toward the empty warehouse district a few blocks away. "...if someone comes after Julio? Then what?"

"Then I shoot them – in the leg. I'm good at it."

"So you've got a pact with a gang." Danny looked hard into the rear view mirror. Shawn looked up at the mirror, into Danny's eyes. Suki looked out the window at nothing, trying, for once, to stay out of the action.

"Yes, I do. I have found, in the past 24 hours, the world is dangerous. Now so am I."

117

"What about the FBI?" asked Suki.

"I want some assurances before I bring them in. First of all, I want protection for you, then immunity for me. I've broken a few laws recently, remember?" Shawn patted the pistol in his belt, reminding her of the string of bodies left behind in the street and at the night club.

Danny drove, getting more and more apprehensive as they got closer to the warehouse district. What started out giving refuge to a friend had turned into a drama involving factions he only wanted to read about. He might see a movie about gangsters and gangs but he didn't want to be in the middle of it. Like it or not, the middle seemed to be where he ended up.

At Shawn's instruction, he pulled around to the back alley. Shawn got out and went up to the broken window. He picked up a length of wood and smashed the remaining piece of glass in, taking out all the shards and pieces with a few deft motions.

"Up you go," he said to Suki. Shawn held out his hands to give Suki a lift up. She got the picture and stepped up into his hands. A moment later, she was through the window.

"Go around, I'll get the door," she said.

Shawn got into the car and pointed down the alley. Danny took the hint and drove to the end, turning right at the street and another right at the corner, pulling up as the garage door was opening. He hadn't yet stopped when Shawn got out to pull the garage door down. He knew little Suki couldn't do it. As he grabbed the door, he cursed not getting an automatic opener.

"But then," thought Shawn "if I did, the electronic opener would still be in my Toyota. Damned if you do and damned if you don't!"

A block away, Coleman watched the warehouse through binoculars. He put down the binoculars and picked up the phone.

"They're back. I said they'd come back. They've got someone with them, a kid, it looks like."

"Good, Coleman. Where are you now?"

"Across the empty lot in the next block."

"Go back up on the roof. Drive them out to us."

Cochran turned off the phone, "We've got them now!"

Linked

"She's in trouble," said Lacra. She had been sitting on the couch at the house in Boyle Heights, looking into space while fighting back tears.

"Yeah, she is." Julio was being agreeable, not agreeing. He sat on the floor not watching the show on TV. His mind was also on Shawn and the girl with the tattoo she didn't ask for.

"No, I mean right now, at this moment, she's in trouble. We should go there."

Julio looked up. For a long time he had suspected Lacra of being in touch with another side of the universe; this confirmed it for him.

"How do you know?" asked Hector.

"I just know. We've got to go."

Lacra got up and walked across the room in a few paces. Having a small stride didn't stand in her way when she had her mind made up. She took a nine-millimeter Baby Eagle out of the desk and put it in her belt at the small of her back.

Julio felt left behind sitting on the floor. He leaped to his feet and covered the distance to the desk in two strides. From the center drawer, he pulled his favorite, the Beretta M9 and stuck it in his belt.

"I'm going to make sure the guy and the Asian girl are OK, and I'm packin' just in case. Who's comin'?" shouted Julio to the assembled crew in the kitchen.

All conversation stopped as butter knives were laid down and thoughts of snacks forgotten. Hector and Jesus were the first out of the door, each trying to take up the lead. The crew filled two cars, scraping the road as they left the driveway in a hurry, sending sparks flying out behind.

On the second floor of the warehouse, Suki sat on the bed, gobbled up by the covers, happy to be warm and dry. She watched Shawn pour the tea, then go to his dresser for a clean shirt. Danny sat at the work bench inspecting Shawn's project. Everything was in its proper place.

Shawn had just slipped on a shirt, blue denim with the Tickleme.com logo, a stylistic cartoon of a giant foot being touched with a feather and a ridiculous face laughing. One day, he thought, people might pay big bucks for an original Tickleme.com shirt. The company was still in the infant stages so the shirt wouldn't have drawn ninety-nine cents on eBay. Still, it was good to not be in someone else's clothes.

Suki didn't have the luxury. She sat on the bed in Danny's clothes while Danny oo'd and ah'd over Shawn's project.

"Programmable, digital amplification and shaping. Speakers by Bose the size of your fist, the whole thing fits in a single box. So with a couple of stands you have all your equipment in the back of your hybrid. And it programs to any amplifier sound, so you can have any amp duplicated."

Danny was impressed. "This is one step beyond, Dude! You can set up for a show with one trip from your car and it looks like you got nothin' til you blast 'em outa their seats with a vintage sound. This is out there!"

"If I could get the backing, I could not only make it work, but put it into production. In fact, I happen to have a warehouse right downstairs. Of course, there is still a little issue of the bass column. I'd like to get one of them."

"But this is doable. Will Bose back you up?"

"I don't know. I haven't asked 'em. I've just been playing with it, trying to get it right."

"Bro, you have it right. This is – well, you got a program to give you all the Line 6 amp options and complete variables of the amps – even the ones not originally part of... but this is essentially..."

A gunshot from the back of the loft and the sound of shattering glass cut Danny off. The bullet flew by Shawn's ear and into a low-hanging support beam. Shawn hit the floor, followed by Danny. Suki rolled off of the bed and dove underneath.

"Back downstairs!" yelled Shawn. "We've got to get out of here!"

"This way," said Danny, pointing around the kitchen to the doorway, avoiding the path of the next shot. Suki and Shawn followed him as another bullet hit the microwave, splintering the glass door into fine shards.

On the roof of the warehouse, Coleman smiled. He holstered his gun and sprinted across the roof and down the aging fire escape to the alley.

Danny took the stairs three at a time and was already at the car. Shawn ran to the garage door, ready to throw it up as soon as he heard the Fit's engine. Suki ran around to the side door, ready to open it and jump in just before Shawn. As soon as Danny started the car, Shawn pulled up on the door. What they saw then froze them in their tracks.

In the street outside, blocking their exit, sat two large sedans, Cochran, Walker and Surroyan standing by them with guns drawn.

Standoff

Shawn drew the nine-millimeter automatic from his belt and stepped in front of Suki, pulling her behind him with his free hand.

Cochran chuckled.

"You're protecting her? She's not the one in harm's way. We want to keep her alive. It's you who's in mortal danger."

Coleman ran up, a thick, black gun in his hand. He was about to speak, something to make the already hopeless situation feel even more hopeless, when a sound distracted them – car wheels squealing.

Behind the four gunmen, a familiar black Cadillac pulled up from one side as a lowered 1965 Chevy Impala screeched to a halt on the other side. Julio's gang sprang from every door. Soon nine gang members, one of them a small girl with piercing eyes and a big gun, surrounded the four gunmen.

The air hung thick for a moment, as the next move was pondered on all sides. Until Surroyan broke the trance.

"I'd like to say something to put this all in perspective, if I may."

Cochran, Coleman and Walker all looked at Surroyan with disbelieving eyes. Shawn wondered what he could possibly say to put it all in perspective. Suki peeked out from behind Shawn and Danny gripped the wheel of the car.

Surroyan turned, pointing his gun at Walker and Cochran. He pulled out a small, black wallet and held a badge high in the air.

"Federal Agent. You are under arrest. Put your guns down and your hands behind your heads. I deputize these men here to aid me in your apprehension and to collect your weapons."

A nervous moment for Julio and his crew passed, replaced by a smile – they were deputized. The mood didn't last long.

Coleman fired first, shooting at Surroyan, who returned the fire, dropping Coleman with a single shot. Cochran raised his gun to Shawn, with a look saying he would not lose the girl again, but Shawn's gun fired first, sending a bullet into Cochran's thigh. It may have saved his life, for as Cochran doubled over in pain, grabbing the gushing wound on his leg, a bullet meant for his heart tore through his right arm. Cochran dropped his gun, crying out in pain.

A dozen shots rang out as Walker spun around, spraying the cars behind him with bullets. Julio stood up and fired back, with better accuracy. Walker fell and Cochran raised his left hand.

"All right!" he yelled. "Enough! I give up."

Coleman and Walker lay dead on the pavement. None of Julio's gang were hit, but all the cars showed bullet holes. In Cochran's car, sitting behind the wheel patiently waiting to be taken into custody, sat Mason, Cochran's right-hand-man. In the middle of it all stood Shawn, his pistol smoking from shooting Cochran. Behind Shawn, Suki held onto his belt and held her breath as well.

"Would you please put these on the fellow in the car?" Surroyan handed a set of handcuffs to Hector, standing close to him.

"You bet!" said Hector. He opened the door and dragged Mason out, cuffing him. "You got the right to remain silent, sucker, and you better do it."

Surroyan cuffed Cochran to the wheel of the car by his good hand. He called in for an ambulance team. When asked if he needed backup, he said, "No, not necessary, we have it covered."

Julio walked up to Shawn, smiling.

"We're deputized," said Julio.

"Yeah, and you did a good job, too."

Aftermath

Danny got out of the car, still shaken. His rear-view mirror had been shattered by Coleman's bullet. He found Shawn holding Suki, who looked like she would never let go of him. Cochran was in custody, sitting in his own car, handcuffed. Surroyan was on the phone; Coleman and Walker lay dead in the street.

The Boyle Heights Lobos congratulated themselves on a job well done. Jesus came up to Danny and slapped him on the back.

"Hey, man, what do you think? We're deputized!"

"Yeah," said Danny, unable to make his mouth work right.

Suki peeled herself away from Shawn as Surroyan came up to them.

"I've got a call in to the local authorities, Sergeant Wentworth will be here soon. He's been on this since you left cars and bodies all over the Los Angeles streets," Surroyan said, a crooked smile softening his features.

"Only in self-defense," said Shawn, hoping to avoid jail.

"I understand. I'll make the point to Wentworth, which will be easier than explaining my backup." Surroyan looked over at the Lobos, standing sentry over the crime scene. "This is one for the books."

"This can't be all there is, just a few men?" asked Suki "There has to be a network, a large support team for such an operation."

"Cochran is the man at the top of this part of it. Now that he's down, my counterparts will handle the rest. The Japanese authorities will move on the Asian contingency. There's just one loose end to tie up." Surroyan looked at Suki.

"Kevin," she said.

"Yes, Kevin. We've yet to find him, but I don't think he's taken it on the fly. He might be hanging out somewhere, feeling happy with himself."

"I had no idea what he was doing," said Suki, still clinging to Shawn.

"I know. It'll all come out now, though. You may have some difficult times coming up. There will be reporters and you'll have to testify."

Suki sputtered a chuckle, "Can't be any worse than what I've been through."

Surroyan looked at Shawn. "Where do you figure in this, champ?"

"Oh, she ran into me on Friday and we thought we'd spend the weekend together," said Shawn, smiling wryly.

"Yeah. Some weekend. I'll take that, if you please." Surroyan indicated the gun.

Shawn handed the nine-mil over. Surroyan took out the magazine and opened the breech, freeing the bullet from the chamber.

"Good shot. You've done that shot before," he said to Shawn.

"A couple of times, it's getting easier." Shawn remembered Rossini and his cousins, recovering in police custody from gunshot wounds. He jerked a thumb at the gang members milling around in the street. "All in self-defense. We've got witnesses."

"Then I'll be out here handling the locals, I hear them coming now," said Surroyan. Sure enough, the sound of a siren was heard in the distance, growing louder.

Lacra came to the door of the garage, pistol still smoking. She looked up at Shawn, put her gun in her coat pocket and reached a hand to Suki.

As Lacra and Suki hugged, Shawn could hear Lacra crying. Suki looked up at Shawn with tears forming in her eyes as well. Shawn stepped back and leaned on the car with Danny. The two of them drew a long breath and took in the crime scene at Shawn's garage door.

"This is not what I expected," yelled Sergeant Wentworth to Shawn as he came into the garage. "Hell, I expected to find you standing over these two, a brace of smoldering pistols in your hands and a dagger in your teeth. Shawn Cauver, I presume."

Shawn nodded, still expecting to be hauled off in cuffs. But the gruff policeman turned to Suki next.

"And this will be the young lady in the middle. We've been looking for you."

Suki turned to Shawn and buried her face in his chest.

"I sure didn't expect to find a local gang lead by an FBI agent. That's a new one. We're gonna need a statement from you two. And I bet it's gonna be a duzzie! Is there someone I can arrest this time?" he asked Surroyan.

"Yes and no. There's two dead bodies over here, a result of the gunfire you were following up," said Surroyan.

Wentworth glanced over and scowled.

"You can have these guys if you like." Surroyan pointed to Cochran and Mason.

"And these?" Wentworth indicated the Boyle Heights Lobos, a group he already knew far too well.

"They're my deputies. They helped me to disarm and apprehend these dangerous criminals. They're to be commended."

Wentworth looked at Surroyan with suspicion, wondering if he was pulling a fast one and getting away with it. Surroyan tried hard not to smile – it would have been rude.

In the distance, another siren signaled the arrival of an ambulance. Wentworth turned again to Shawn.

"So your Toyota's sitting in our lot, full of holes?"

"Yes, sir."

"Well, it's shot. You need a new one."

Wentworth stomped off to his car, spitting orders to his uniformed officers.

Surroyan just smiled. Yes, there would be a mountain of paperwork and a room full of techs testing guns to find out just who shot who. Somehow, he didn't think it mattered anymore.

C. J. Abbot

Statements

Surroyan took Shawn and Suki upstairs to get their statements for his report.

"I'll copy Wentworth for the police report. You won't have to go downtown. You've been through enough. The gang will be hard to explain. It'll be hard to balance out the laws they broke today just by showing up with guns." Surroyan smiled. He had no intention of letting the police press charges.

"They saved the day," said Suki.

"Well I know, and I won't forget it, either. But I owe you a debt of gratitude, miss. I've been after this ring for a long time. I've been on the fringes until now. It was your abduction and," he directed to Shawn, "the trail of bodies and shot-up cars you left all over town – that brought me in close enough to make a real arrest and have it stick."

"What about Kevin?" asked Suki.

"He'll be arrested for kidnapping and his part in slave trafficking. His conspiracy in this puts him in a bad spot. I wouldn't count on him coming to Thanksgiving dinner any time soon."

Suki managed a small chuckle, more like a squeak.

She never wanted to see Kevin again. She hoped he would go away for a long time. Her attention went to the pain on her back from the horishi's needle. She would have a reminder of her ordeal for the remainder of her life.

"Hey, man, slick!" came a voice from the stair as Julio stepped onto the landing. The entire gang was behind him, having given their statements to the police. Wentworth let them go with a warning not to be seen with their weapons again, bringing a muffled laugh.

"Give us a minute, guys, while I get a statement here," said Surroyan.

"You got it, chief!" said Julio, taking an interest in the work bench. Danny ran to intercept him, hoping to explain the project before it fell into the hands of the uninitiated.

After the statements were taken, Surroyan put them into a leather folder and stood up with a 'good-bye' feeling.

"You two have pulled it off. Well done."

"Thanks. If you weren't there, it could have ended badly," said Shawn over a handshake. Suki interrupted with a large hug to Surroyan. On the verge of becoming emotional himself, Surroyan gave a small wave and loped down the stairs.

The gang members got it and filed down the stairs, calling Danny and Shawn "Bro" as they went.

Julio lingered, wanting a moment with Shawn.

"Brothers-in-arms," said Julio.

"Thank you, my friend," said Shawn, pulling Julio to him. They each socked the other on the shoulder and Julio departed down the stair.

Shawn turned around to see Lacra and Suki holding each other, both crying. Suki pulled back to look into Lacra's eyes.

"You shot him?"

"Bet your sweet ass I did!" said Lacra, with the eyes of a huntress.

"You'll have to teach me how to do that," said Suki, making Lacra smile. She nodded and both girls smiled, then returned to hugging.

Danny was still at the workbench. Shawn ambled over to him.

"I think I can see where you went wrong on this," said Danny, turning he attention to the workbench.

131

"Wrong? What do you mean wrong?"

"Well, looks like you're stuck on this step," Danny pointed at the guitar.

Lacra turned to go down the stairs with Suki looking after her. She then turned to Shawn and Danny, watching them haggle over the project spread across the workbench.

Until that moment, there had been just one thing to do: stay out of the clutches of the bad men in suits. Now there was a thousand things to do and she didn't feel in fit shape to do any of them.

"I have to call my father. He'll be a wreck! My mother too. They'll want to meet you and have dinner – lots of dinners. Get ready."

"OK, lots of dinners. Check!" said Shawn, looking over at three cups of tea they never got to drink.

Suki went to the phone and it was an hour before they had her attention again.

"I spoke with my uncle in Tokyo. I'll be going to stay with him a while. He'll be here in a day or so to take me back. It's best." Suki sat on the bed next to Shawn. She put her arms around him. "But I'm going to miss you."

A Visit from Surroyan

A month had gone by. Danny and Shawn sat at the workbench putting the finishing touches on the project Shawn had been working on since he first moved in.

Surroyan had called to say he was on his way over. When the knock on the door came, Shawn got up from the workbench to answer the door downstairs.

"Agent Surroyan," said Shawn, opening the door wide.

"Shawn. You're looking well." Agent Surroyan came in, glancing at the loading area sporting two Honda Fits, Danny's blue one and a new red one. "You got a new car?"

"Yeah, well, like the sergeant said, the other one was shot."

"How's Suki?" asked Surroyan as they walked up the stairs.

"She's better, recovering. She's on her way to Tokyo, staying with her uncle. He has people who can remove the tattoo. She wants to put this behind her."

"I don't blame her. Hi Danny!" said Surroyan, stepping onto the landing.

"Agent Surroyan, how goes the investigation? Are they giving you any trouble?"

"Cochran gave us everything we need and we can't shut Mason up. Our counterparts closed down the Asian organization at the same time. This might have taken months if Suki hadn't gotten away from them. She would have disappeared into a world unknown to us. As it was, chasing her was their downfall."

"Thank you for your handling of the final standoff."

133

"Yeah, flying by the seat of my pants."

Surroyan looked at the workbench, noting changes in the place. Against the wall a pile of boxes, some marked "Bose" and others marked "Fender."

"You got your backing? You're going into production?"

"Yeah, my uncle came through with some money so we're going into production. In fact, we're waiting for our new associate now, a friend of mine."

"Well, I won't stay, I just wanted to see you were OK and let you know we're wrapping this thing up. You'll be called to testify."

"I am at your service," said Shawn.

"And me," added Danny, not wanting to be left out. "Those guys shot at me too. The insurance company didn't believe a bullet had come through my car."

"I'll send you the police report. Oh, they're tearing down the night club. It's been condemned."

"Good. It should be," said Shawn.

A loud knock from below caught Shawn's attention.

"That's my cue," said Surroyan. He shook Shawn's hand and Danny's, then walked toward the stairs with Shawn behind him.

"Don't be a stranger, you know where we are," said Shawn at the door.

"No problem. You'll be invited to a ceremony, an award for my deputies."

Shawn and Surroyan both smiled as Shawn opened the door. There was Carrie, holding a giant bag of popcorn. She smiled too, as everyone was doing so. Surroyan nodded to her as he went out.

Shawn stepped aside, indicating for her to come in. At the curb sat Carrie's Chevy Malibu. Shawn looked at it and smiled; no one in Malibu drove one.

"Yours?" said Carrie, indicating the two Hondas.

"One of them, come on up."

"And who's your friend?" Carrie looked back towards Surroyan as she followed Shawn up the broad stairway.

"It's a long story – but an interesting one, one in which you had a small part. In fact, you – well, I'll fill you in. Come and meet Danny."

Shawn took Carrie over to the work bench with Danny hard at work with the soldering gun. She looked around the loft with wide eyes, unable to take it in all at once.

"Danny, this is Carrie. I mentioned her. Carrie, meet Danny."

"Shawn speaks highly of you. I've been looking forward to meeting you." Danny reached a hand.

"Thanks, glad to be here," said Carrie, taking the offered hand.

"And this," said Shawn, pointed to the work bench, the stacks of guitars and boxes of electronic gear, "is your new workplace. Welcome to the company."

"Thank you. This is gonna be fun!"

Shawn nodded, listening for a moment. The rain had finally stopped.

# # #

Tattooed Angel is the first book by C. J. Abbot.
We hope to see other work by this author soon.
Midnight Whistler Publishers